Steve Gooch

The Women Pirates
Ann Bonney and Mary Read

Pluto  Plays

To Jane

The Women Pirates Ann Bonney and Mary Read

Plays can have unlikely origins. *Ann and Mary*, as my women-pirates play was originally called, began in 1969 when a small theatre company I'd been working with said they wanted a play about cops and robbers. Two women and three men. I wasn't keen on the kind of satirical portrait of the contemporary copper which was popular at that time. Nor for that matter was I sold on the romantic outlaw-hero idea. I felt the theme needed a context of real historical and social conditions. So I began digging in the popular historical literature of outlaws to find a source which had the kind of resonance I was looking for. I wanted a story which not only offered a socially critical or satirical perspective of the law, but one which also spoke positively of the creative potential in the people opposing it.

I was staying one weekend with a radical feminist friend when at breakfast a tiny booklet called something like 'Famous Outlaws' fell out of the shredded wheat packet. In it was a brief account of the lives of Ann Bonney and Mary Read. The friend and I both found their story so rich in the variety of levels at which it exposed the superficiality of the legal system, particularly towards women in an even more patriarchal society than today's, that it seemed a good vehicle for the play. Lengthier consultation in, amongst other books, Captain Johnson's *The Robberies and Murders of the Most Notorious Pirates* confirmed that original impression.

By the time I'd got stuck into the play, however, the theatre company had run out of money and the play was spreading in size. Both the broad panorama which the women's lives spanned and the need to pin down its social and historical conditions meant it had to be a big play. A dozen women characters, a couple of dozen men, all in costume with multiple sets and songs. Nabisco had a lot to answer for.

What was more, the play's subject-matter was changing. It became clear in research that all the places through which Ann and Mary pursued their personal odysseys were places where the European empire-builders of the eighteenth century were clashing: Ireland, Flanders, Carolina, the Caribbean. The geographical span of their lives reproduced the economic links and political hot-spots of their age. It was as if these two women were fleeing not only their sex-role stereotypes and the law, but the development of British imperialism itself. Furthermore, what brought them together was a small 'alternative society' of anti-colonial rebels – the pirate community in what are now the Bahamas. Sort of eighteenth century Yippies.

And in learning about how that 'alternative' pirate community organised itself, I began to find the means to express the positive side of the play. Ann and Mary don't just reject and break away from the rules of conventional society, they take part in an attempt to make a new way of life. They become potential law-makers as well as law-breakers. And here the 'no-women' rule of the otherwise democratic pirate-crews afforded an interesting parallel with the tendency towards sexism of some of today's 'alternative' institutions.

By the early 1970s the play had gone through several drafts, won an award, and several theatre managements had expressed interest in doing it. But big plays are difficult financially, and we were into the recession. One by one, mooted productions fell through because of lack of money. The play took on the character of a quest for myself and director Ron Daniels, who championed it consistently for five years.

And because of this long history, each successive draft of the play came to represent a stage in the process of learning which working in the theatre can mean. New ideas and techniques were tried out, adding insights as it went along, stripping away what was unnecessary. Throughout this process however the play's origins in alternative theatre and its premise of a more active and engaged relationship to its audience remained consistent. And the central theme of liberation from ruling-class law and morality has developed, relating to men as well as women and also to the struggle for freedom within the institutions we create to combat that law.

Looking back now, I'm aware of how a play which started out as an historical cops and robbers play from a feminist and anti-imperialist view has in fact increasingly become a reflection on the period during which it was written, a play about the possibilities for freedom in an alternative movement, its origins, its experiments, its weaknesses. Perhaps only in the late 1970s can we begin to get a bead on the late 1960s.

Steve Gooch

The Women Pirates Ann Bonney and Mary Read: was first performed by the Royal Shakespeare Company at the Aldwych Theatre, London, on 31 July 1978. The cast was as follows:

Mabel/Old Woman in public	Denyse Alexander
Ginny/Young Whore	Jill Baker
Polly/Mary	Charlotte Cornwell
Mrs Read/Old Whore	Yvonne Coulette
Elizabeth/Creole Woman	Deidra Morris
Peg/Ann	Diana Quick
Forbes	John Burgess
Deane	Peter Clough
Corporal/Earl	Ron Cook
Vosquin/Blackie	Charles Dance
Kendal/Davies	Alan David
Stroller/Norris	Jeffery Dench
Pierre/Eaton	Philip Dunbar
Bonney/Soldier 2	David Hobbs
Sergeant/Howell	Geoffrey Hutchings
Thomas/Charley/Fetherstone	Jeffrey Kissoon
Harwood	Ian McNiece
Will/Spenlow/Lawes	Edwin Richfield
Barnet	Stephen Jenn
Rackham	Nigel Terry
Man in public	Michael Hall
Soldier 1	Bille Brown

Directed by Ron Daniels
Designed by Chris Dyer and Di Seymour
Music by Guy Woolfenden
Lighting by Leo Leibovici
Fights arranged by B. H. Barry

All the characters in the play can be played by a minimum of 17 actors (the minimum required for the scene in Pierre's Café), although this leaves extremely quick changes for the Mrs Read/Mabel and Elizabeth/Young Whore doubles, which can be divided again as indicated below.

EARLY SCENES		CAFÉ SCENE		LAST SCENE
Poll		Mary		Mary
Peg		Ann		Ann
Mrs Read/Mabel		Old Whore		Old Woman in public
Ginny/Elizabeth (Scene 5)		Young Whore		Creole Woman
		Rackham		Rackham
Forbes*		Forbes*		Forbes*
Bonney		Bonney ⎱ (Deane in Scenes		Deane
Jules ⎤		Pierre ⎰ 8 and 9)		
		Blackie ⎤ ⎰ (Eaton in Scene 9)		Eaton
Sergeant*		Stroller* ⎬ ⎱ (Sailor in Scene 9)		
		Spenlow* ⎦		
Will Cormac*		Harwood* ⎤		Norris* ⎤
		Fetherstone* ⎰		Lawes*
Thomas the servant	(Charley the Indian in Scene 4)	Howell		Soldier 1
				Barnet
Kendal		Barnet		Soldier 2
		Davies		Man in public
Corporal ⎦		Earl ⎦		

* indicates parts played preferably by older actors

List of characters

Singers

Mrs Read, Mary's grandmother
Alexander Forbes, a planter
Thomas, a negro servant
Poll, Mary's mother
Ginny, Poll's friend
Mary as a little girl

Will Cormac, Ann's father
Peg, Ann's mother
Mabel Cormac, Will's wife

Sergeant
Corporal
Jules Vosquin
Mary Read

Fortesque Kendal, a suitor
Ann Bonney
Charley, her Indian friend
James Bonney, a smuggler

Elizabeth, a serving girl

Pierre, café proprietor
Old Whore ⎫
Young Whore ⎬ 'regulars' at Pierre's
Stroller ⎭
Tom Spenlow, a sailor
Thomas Earl ⎫
John Davies ⎮
John Howell ⎮
Blackie ⎬ pirates
Noah Harwood ⎮
George Fetherstone ⎭
Jack 'Calico' Rackham, pirate captain
Captain Barnet, officer in King's Navy

Thomas Deane, a navigating officer

John Eaton, a turtler
A Sailor

Sir Nicholas Lawes ⎫
William Norris ⎬ planters
Creole Woman
Soldiers
Men and women in public at trial

ACT I

No set throughout the play, but as a backcloth, a large and colourful map of the western hemisphere. On it the countries where the play's scenes take place are marked vividly, as are the main products of their economies. Solid three-dimensional props then serve to set scenes.

The SINGERS *come on. They sing:*

Singers Sugar and spice and all things nice
That's what England was made of.
Cotton and tea and rubber and rice
From all around the world.
Sugar and spice and all things nice
But not for little girls.

> Now Mary Read was a pirate
> And so was a girl called Ann.
> They could fight and kill as easy
> As many a muscle-bound man.
> For both girls were born out of wedlock,
> And because that's considered a sin,
> Once they were put outside the law
> It was hard to get back in.

Sugar and spice and all things nice
That's what the rich were made of.
They drew the line and didn't think twice
All around the world.
Sugar and spice and all things nice
But not for little girls.

> Now when Mary was a toddler
> Her mother was very poor.
> So to help keep ends together
> She decided to bend the law.
> But children are tender creatures
> And boy from girl can be hard to tell.
> So while Mary's mother bent the law
> She bent her daughter's life as well.

Sugar and spice and all things nice
That's what this world was made of.
But it came at too steep a price

> For these little girls.
> No sugar, no spice, they had to think twice:
> About another world.

The SINGERS *announce* . . .

1696 THE READ FAMILY'S RESIDENCE IN PLYMOUTH

. . . and go off.

Lush furnishing.

MRS READ *comes on to* ALEXANDER FORBES.

Mrs Read Mr Forbes, how nice to see you in England again!

Forbes (*shaking hands*) I'm never away longer than I can help, Ma'am.

Mrs Read From us in Devon, or is London the real attraction?

Forbes I'm afraid it's duty more than pleasure brings me this time, Mrs Read. The situation on the island's become so extreme, a visit home was imperative.

Mrs Read Has there been some trouble?

Forbes Disorder on the plantations and piracy at sea. And they're not unconnected.

Mrs Read You're still losing men then?

Forbes Our indentured labour. They're sent to us in Jamaica on two- or three-year contracts rather than go to prison here. Then they find the plantations too hard for their liking, so they run off to join the pirates.

Mrs Read An expanding population, by all accounts.

Forbes And all stealing our sugar.

Mrs Read With foreign help no doubt.

Forbes That's why the new Bill's so important. If English goods can only be transported in English ships, we may get things under control again.

Mrs Read Are we badly affected?

Forbes There'll still be a dividend, Mrs Read. But our main need is more capital.

Mrs Read Which is why you're here.

Forbes I have to talk to our investors, of course. And to Parliament about the Bill. But I also need to make contact with more magistrates. They must send us more labour. I understand you have an acquaintance in Bristol.

Mrs Read Cousin Edward. Would you like an introduction?

Forbes That's very kind. It'll take a big drive if we're to reverse this pirate menace.

Mrs Read About the other matter, Mr Forbes: I'd need some assurance of course before I committed myself.

Forbes The crop's there for the taking, Ma'am. If we get our labour and the new Act goes through, this coming year could be better than ever.

THOMAS, *a perfectly liveried negro servant, appears. He stands to one side.*

Mrs Read Excuse me. – Thomas?

Servant I'm sorry to disturb you, Ma'am. Your daughter-in-law. She says she has an appointment.

Mrs Read So she has. Will you stay for tea, Mr Forbes?

Forbes Delighted, Ma'am.

He stands.

Mrs Read Thank you, Thomas.

The SERVANT *goes.*

Forbes One of ours?

Mrs Read Trinidad in fact. All of a sudden they've become fashionable. – Let me show you through.

They go off. The SERVANT *comes back with* POLLY READ, GINNY *and* MARY *as a little girl, dressed in a sailor suit. The* SERVANT *goes.*

Ginny D'you see that, Poll!

Polly Black. From Africa.

Ginny An' dressed up all fine!

Polly Still a slave though.

Pause. They look around.

Ginny Grand, en it.

Polly Where's it all come from, Ginny, that's what I'd like to know.

She straightens MARY's *suit.*

Ginny What you goin' a say, Poll?

Polly I'll tell her she's a boy.

Ginny That all?

Polly I'll tell her little Mary's little Mark.

Ginny She don't look much like a boy.

Polly She's got her sailor-suit. Remind the old girl of her son. (*Ironic.*) My dear husband Jack, departed on the high seas for ever. I'll tell her she's little Marky, her grandson, an' I've come for his inheritance.

Ginny Marky's dead though.

Polly No good to me that way.

Ginny It's not honest, Poll.

Polly So what? The old girl can afford it. Why should I rot in the country while his Dad lives it up on the high seas?

Ginny They always said Jack got drowned.

Polly Sailors don't get drowned 'less they want to.

Ginny Anythin' could've happened. He might've been kidnapped. Set to work on a plantation.

Polly He's havin' it off in some pirate dive right now, I bet you.

Ginny It's happened before.

Polly Either way I'm left holdin' the baby.

Ginny You shouldn't have married a sailor.

Polly Everyone tells you after, don't they.

Ginny Why'd you go an' have another anyway?

Polly Two months married an' your old man disappears on you? I was just gettin' a taste for it.

Ginny You devil!

Polly It was the cock I needed, girl, not the bloody egg.

Ginny We're goin' a miss you, Poll.

Polly Yeh, I bet.

MRS READ *approaches.*

Ginny That her now?

Polly (*to* LITTLE MARY) Now remember what I told you, Mary. Keep your tongue still. If Grandma finds out you're a girl, you can say bye-bye to your nice new pink dress.

MRS READ *comes up to them.*

Mrs Read Polly, Ginny! You got here safely.

Ginny Ma'am.

She curtseys.

Polly I brought the child, Mrs Read.

Mrs Read It's not a girl, I hope. All my children seem able to produce is grand-daughters. Five already and they all want money for them. After all, it is our *men* who rule the waves.

Polly Beg pardon, Ma'am?

Mrs Read The new Act, my dear. We can't have the French and Spanish profiting from our pioneers.

Ginny Is that what they're doin' then?

Mrs Read That's why we're at war, dear.

Ginny All I know is, it makes everythin' go up.

Mrs Read Yes, wars *are* expensive, it's true. But worth it in the long run. There's much more money around now.

Polly If there is, we ain' seen much of it.

Ginny Seven bad summers in a row, Ma'am. Price a grain up an' down like a yo-yo. An' since you enclosed the common ground, we ain' even got that bit extra comin' in. The little we got over we have to sell in town.

Mrs Read Things can't be too bad. If you've a little over, Ginny.

Ginny 'Cept you're puttin' the rent up.

Mrs Read But everything's going up, Ginny. That's the way of things! The price of your lovely eggs too, I'm sure. We're in the same boat on that score.

Polly No, Ma'am. You're in your mansion an' they're in a cottage that's too small.

Ginny We can't afford to keep Poll with us no more, Mrs R.

Polly That's why I brought little Marky, Ma'am. I thought, with the money comin' to Jack, we could rent a place in town. Little draper's be nice.

Mrs Read I doubt if Jack's money would stretch to that, Polly.

Polly Just so I'm not a burden on Ginny.

MRS READ *turns her attention to* LITTLE MARY.

Mrs Read He doesn't look much like my Jack.

Polly It's the light, Ma'am. He takes more after my side.

Mrs Read The pretty face, you mean.

Ginny That's the country air, Ma'am. Good for the complexion.

Mrs Read (*to* LITTLE MARY) Hello, little man!

LITTLE MARY *doesn't answer.*

I haven't seen you since you were a little tiny baby, have I?

No response.

Mmm?

No response.

Doesn't say much, does he.

Polly Livin' in the country does that, Ma'am. He gets on better with cows.

Mrs Read Really. (*To* LITTLE MARY.) Naughty Mummy didn't write and tell us where she was, did she.

Polly I'm not one for letter-writin', Ma'am.

Mrs Read Only comes to see me when she wants money.

Polly If there's money due to Jack, Mrs Read, the child's got a right to it.

Mrs Read As long as it is Jack's child. You were away a long time. You could've had two or three more and we'd be none the wiser.

Polly I didn't come here to be insulted, Ma.

Mrs Read I'm sorry, Polly, but the family were very upset when you went away. They're not the most trusting people.

Polly I didn't want to see no-one after Jack died. You know how it is.

Pause.

Ginny He's a fine boy, Ma'am. Always on the go. All we can do to keep up with him.

Mrs Read He's small for five though.

Polly What you call a slow developer.

Mrs Read (*to* LITTLE MARY) You are a little boy, are you?

LITTLE MARY *doesn't answer.*

Polly He was last time I looked.

Mrs Read You haven't thought of marrying again?

Polly Fellas won't look twice if you got a kid.

Mrs Read You could always let me look after him. It's a long time since I had a baby to bath.

Polly (*quick*) I couldn't do that, Ma'am.

Mrs Read Why not? He'd have a good home. You'd be free to find a husband.

Polly Break my heart to be separated from him, Ma, honest.

MRS READ *takes* LITTLE MARY *in her arms.*

Mrs Read You're not a little girl, are you?

Polly I had him, Ma, I should know.

Mrs Read I had four of my own, Polly. I can still tell the difference, even if I'm past enjoying it.

Polly If I couldn't, Ma, it'd be a miracle I had him in the first place.

Mrs Read (*looking* LITTLE MARY *closely up and down*) You're not a little impostor, are you?

Polly No brand on his backside if that's what you're lookin' for.

Mrs Read It's important to be sure, Polly. It could work out hard on the child.

Polly Have a look then.

Mrs Read I'm sorry?

Polly Have a feel. Only way to tell.

Mrs Read If we can't be honest, Poll, at least we can be decent.

Polly I want to bring this kid up decent.

Mrs Read You realise of course, if I give you this money, Ginny's rent will absolutely have to go up. The market's much less certain than it was. Three companies have collapsed in Exeter in the last six months.

Pause.

Polly You're sayin' if I don't ask for that money Ginny's rent can stay the same.

Mrs Read Not for ever, but I wouldn't want to be uncharitable. That's why I give to our school for the needy. One should always help those who can't help themselves. Especially as there are some who'll help themselves anyway. Aren't there, Polly.

Polly It's one or other of us, Gin.

Pause.

Ginny You must leave the farm, Poll.

Mrs Read That's settled then. A crown a week from the inheritance for the proper education of Jack's boy. But only Jack's boy. Any others you have, you must bear the cost of yourself. Is that clear?

Polly Yes, Ma'am.

Mrs Read In all fairness to my other grandchildren, I can't say more than that. Do you understand me, Polly?

Polly Very good of you, Ma'am, I'm sure.

Mrs Read Well at least someone's happy. We'll talk about your rent another time, Ginny. If you'll excuse me, I have an important guest.

She goes.

Polly No more pink dresses for you, Mark Read.

They go. The SINGERS *come on and sing:*

Singers Now the sins of the parent, they tell us,
Are visited on the child.
If the mum's a bit of a goer
No wonder the kid turns out wild.
For children are tender creatures
And boy from girl can be hard to tell.
And while Mary's mother raised her 'boy'
Ann's father was raising hell.

But it takes two to tell what's right and wrong.
You can draw or cross the line.
And if morals make for sinners,
It's laws that make for crime.

For in Ireland Ann Bonney's father
Was in trouble with the wife.
With his mistress Peggy Brennan
He was planning to lead a new life.
But his wife was just like England,
Mabel Cormac was her name
And though Will said 'Get off my back'
She clung on just the same.

The SINGERS *announce . . .*

1706 CORK, IN IRELAND

. . . and go off.

Room in a small house. WILLIAM CORMAC *is sitting at a table, doing his accounts.* PEG *is packing a trunk. They don't see* MABEL CORMAC *come in.*

Peg Shall I pack the curtains, Will? Can we take them with us?
Will Yes, dear.
Peg And the cutlery?
Will Yes.
Mabel You're an evil swine, Will Cormac.
Will (*looks up*) Who let you in?
Peg Not me, Will.
Mabel The door was open.
Will My God but it's a terrible thing when a man can't leave his wife and settle to his middle age in peace without she's bursting in his door every five minutes.

Mabel It's not every five minutes, Will, and I've come for a special reason which you well know.

Will Do I now?

Mabel In your heart of hearts, yes.

Will Do I have some special kind of guilt about me now that I can fathom the mind of a woman I could never understand in the fifteen long years I lived with her?

Mabel Would it be some kind of guilt I wonder to be living openly with a slut of a maid for whom God eternally damn me that I took her on in the first place.

Peg I am not a slut, Mrs Cormac.

Mabel Or to proclaim to the world that out of the kindness of your heart you've taken in a nephew to train as your clerk, and that nephew all the time none other than this slattern's bastard daughter.

Will So you've found out at last. The wonder is, it took you so long.

Peg I am not a slattern, Mrs Cormac, and the child's name is Ann.

Mabel All it does have for a name, no doubt. And even that after the damn Queen of England.

Will Is it only to slander me you've come, Mabel? If so, you can go. I've heard it all before.

Mabel Run away, you mean. Like yourselves.

Will Or like our Irish soldiers at the Boyne. If this country can't defend itself from being bled to poverty by the English, it can't expect my loyalty.

Mabel Loyalty was never a quality you held in abundance, William. Nor, it seems, shame.

Will Woman, I'm as sensitive to the gossiping tongues of County Cork as you are. Hasn't my practice fallen around my ears on account of them, and that my only means of supporting this family?

Mabel No more than a turncoat protestant adulterer deserves!

Will Mabel, if the English invader won't allow Catholics to practise law in their own country, I am indeed what you call me. But in name only.

Peg We still have the candles and the crucifix, Ma'am. But we observe in secret.

She packs them.

Mabel Do you still have a priest though?

Will Our faith is in the Great Priest, Mabel. That's why I'm shipping myself, this good woman and our child to the New World, where they say a man can at least breathe freely the air God gave him.

Peg Are we taking the lamp, William?

Will No, dear.

Mabel America now, is it? Where you'll no doubt *freely* raise the bastard of this wanton trash on my mother's money.

Peg I am not wanton trash, Mrs Cormac. – Lift up, Will.

Will Yes, dear.

He lifts his books. PEG *takes the tablecloth, packs it and goes.*

Mabel All the time heaping more shame on the poor loving creature that called herself your wife.

Will Is that poor loving creature by any chance threatening now to take away money her mother explicitly left to me?

Mabel My mother explicitly left you nothing but what was meant for our children—mortified as she was by her son's refusal to be reconciled to his wife, and him the guilty party in the first place.

Will Me the guilty party? Wasn't it yourself gave birth to identical twins two months before your mother's death, there being no cause that I had anything to do with why you should.

Mabel You'll have forgotten no doubt the night I returned from my mother's, having lain five weeks sick with fever, and never in all that time receiving a visit from yourself.

Will I had my practice to think of.

Mabel And strange practice it was too. For wasn't I lying in an empty house when a certain prosperous and respected citizen came lusting into his servant's bedroom where I was sleeping for certain suspicions I'd had, and mindless of his wife's return and insensible to her difference from his mistress, screw the senses out of me, crying 'Peg, Peg, you do it wonderful!'

Will My God.

Mabel Then crawl back to his cot and sleep till lunchtime the next day.

Will That was you?

Mabel And with all that to accuse me of infidelity!

Will The devious paths of your mind never cease to amaze me, Mabel. Why didn't you tell me before?

Mabel The hope was, the shock of it might kill you.

Will The twins are my children then.

Mabel You have no right to them, and my mother's money should be theirs.

Will I'll make a deed out tonight. My sorrow is I didn't know this before. You're a deceitful Medea of a woman, Mabel. You let me continue in the belief of your infidelity, when a simple word of truth could have saved us all. I shall take Peg and Ann to Carolina and put as much distance between us as is healthy.

Mabel I hope your boat sinks.

Will Will that be all now?

Mabel It will.

Will Goodbye then.

He offers her his hand.

Mabel (*taking his hand*) God knows how the poor child will turn out.

They go off. The SINGERS *come on and sing:*

> Yes, the sins of the parent, they tell us
> Are visited on the child.
> If the dad's a bit of a goer
> No wonder the kid turns out wild.
> And the Mother England that in Ireland
> Made an outcast for life,
> In Flanders turns the fields to mud,
> A soldier to a wife.
>
> For it takes two to tell what's right and wrong.
> You can draw or cross the line.
> And if men can make girls women, it's
> Women make man-kind.
>
> For it's a man's life in the army,
> Or so the posters say.
> But a girl who's been brought up to it's
> As good as a man any day.
> So Mary joined the army
> And excelled in every way,
> Till she fell in love with her corporal,
> And found the part too hard to play.

They announce . . .

1711 FLANDERS

. . . and go off.

An army camp. A tent. Accoutrements hung up outside. SERGEANT *and* CORPORAL.

Sergeant What would you call these brasses, Corporal?
Corporal Dirty, Sergeant.
Sergeant And these leathers?
Corporal Unpolished.
Sergeant Whose are they?
Corporal Mark Read's.
Sergeant And what is Mark Read?
Corporal A soldier.
Sergeant Would you call these brasses and leathers the accoutrements of a soldier?
Corporal I would not, Sergeant.

Pause.

Sergeant I don't understand. In an age where the NCO struggles daily to train up recruited riff-raff to protect the wealth won for our proud nation by its pioneers abroad, Mark Read was one of my shinin' examples.

Corporal He was certainly that, Sergeant.

Sergeant A model of the New Soldier, that glorious tradition started by the great Cromwell which our commander Mr Churchill – now the Duke of Marlborough – has taken over so we can paste Catholic dagoes from here to the West Indies.

Corporal And back.

Sergeant And back. – His discipline a completely undeserved tribute to those incompetent amateurs, his officers, he was always first into battle, always first on parade, his brasses glintin' proudly in the sun, leathers supple like a fish's back. Canvas clean, tent-pegs bang on thirty degrees, ropes taut. (*Pause.*) Now look at it. Brasses green, leathers all mildew, leaf-mould on his canvas, pegs all anyhow. What's come over him?

Corporal He's in love, Sergeant.

Sergeant I didn't hear that. (*Pause.*) Where *is* Read?

Corporal Fightin' the French.

Sergeant Which company's he in?

Corporal Ours.

Sergeant Are you fightin' the French?

Corporal No.

Sergeant Am I?

Corporal No.

Sergeant So why the fuck's Read fightin' 'em?

Corporal He went off with Vosquin, Sergeant. The Flemish corporal. The Dutch were called in 'count of a surprise French attack at Aubigny. Read went with 'em.

Sergeant Again?

Corporal You can't separate 'em.

Sergeant This is a war we're fightin', not a men's doubles. The Dutch are our allies, not our tennis partners. We tolerate them as our comrades-in-arms because it's their country we're layin' waste to in order to show the French who's boss in Europe. Just because Read's sharin' a tent with one of the evil-smellin' bastards don't mean he's got to fight his battles for him.

Corporal No, Sergeant.

Sergeant Means we're short of tents.

Corpral Right.

Sergeant I thought I explained that to him. Things go astray in the army. Tents, uniforms, men – it's part of the way of life. So due to a traditional oversight on the part of the Quartermaster, four tents were accidentally sold off to a farmer in Ghent to protect his hay harvest durin' the rainy season.

Corporal Correct.

Sergeant So four men had to suffer the inconvenience of sharin' with the

Dutch. Read volunteered. He'd served with the infantry, spoke Dutch. He knew the position.

Corporal You explained it very carefully.

Sergeant It's no worse than officers takin' bribes for commissions. How else is a man to maintain the standard of livin' to which he's accustomed?

Corporal Will you shoot him, Sergeant?

Sergeant I couldn't do that. We need good men. An' shootin' 'em isn't the best way of keepin' 'em. Read's been commended in the field. Nearly made officer when he was in the infantry.

Corporal Didn't have the quality, eh Sergeant?

Sergeant No, didn't have the money.

Corporal It's Vosquin's fault anyway. These foreigners are all the same.

Sergeant Not so, Corporal. The French are all the same, 'cos they're the enemy. And a bigger bunch of cowardly perverts I have yet to lay eyes on. Tryin' to squeeze us out of our hard-won colonies. The Dutch on the other hand are currently our allies. So like all men, except the enemy, they have their good and their bad.

Corporal Vosquin's a Fleming, Sergeant.

Sergeant The distinction I'm afraid is lost on me, Corporal. You say he follows Read everywhere?

Corporal No, Read follows him.

MARY *comes on, supporting* JULES VOSQUIN *who has been wounded in the foot.*

Sergeant I could understand if it was the other way round.

Mary Steady.

Sergeant What's this?

Corporal Read, Sergeant. With the Dutchman.

Sergeant Read, why are you clutchin' that Dutchman?

Mary He's wounded, Sergeant.

Corporal Call that a wound?

Mary He can't walk on it.

Corporal He's not even tryin'.

Jules You try treading on it.

Corporal That an offer, Vosquin?

Sergeant A wound like that wouldn't seriously impede an English soldier, Vosquin.

Jules Got wings up your arses, have you?

Sergeant That part of the Englishman's anatomy hold a particular fascination for you, Dutchman?

Jules We *Flemings* call it the English disease.

Corporal Raised your hopes, did they.

MARY *puts* JULES *down on a bed just inside the tent.*

Sergeant We're worried about you, Read.

Corporal He's been neglectin' his accoutrements, Vosquin. The Sergeant feels he's bein' put upon.

Jules I don't ask him to ride with me.

Corporal Your natural charm, is it.

Sergeant Nothin' worryin' you, Read? Everythin' all right at home?

Mary I ran away from home.

Sergeant Health? Mustn't be shy, you know. First sign of anythin', off to the surgeon.

Mary I'm fine.

Sergeant You were a footboy for a French lady, then a cabin-boy before you joined up, right?

Mary You've got a good memory.

Sergeant You didn't steal anythin'?

Mary No.

Sergeant Why you tryin' to get yourself killed then? No-one's askin' you to ride with the Dutch.

Jules Mark, some water please.

Mary I . . . couldn't let him go on his own.

Sergeant Why? He's old enough to find his way. You don't have to hold his hand.

Mary We work better as a pair.

Sergeant I've never seen him come on *our* parties.

Mary Can I get him some water?

Sergeant There's rumours about you two. You don't want things like that said about you, do you?

Jules Could somebody get me some water!

Sergeant Corporal, get Vosquin water.

Corporal Me?

Sergeant Now!

Corporal Sergeant.

CORPORAL *goes.* SERGEANT *takes* MARY *to one side.*

Sergeant The men think you're mad, Read, riskin' your neck to fight with this Dutchman. He's a lousy soldier. You might as well let him get what's comin' to him an' have the tent to yourself.

Mary I couldn't do that.

Sergeant You're makin' a fool of yourself over this, Soldier. You've got to decide whose side you're on.

Mary The Dutch are on our side.

Sergeant They're sayin' that now. Fifty years ago they coveted our trade like everyone else.

Mary They're fightin' the French, same as us.

Sergeant Not with my men they're not! Fraternity has its limits, understood?

Mary Sergeant.

Sergeant That uniform's a privilege. We've only had it four years, and a lot of high-placed people went to a lot of trouble to get it for us. Understood?

Mary Sergeant.

Sergeant Get your gear cleaned up then, and that tent. I shall be back later, and I want to see that canvas clean and those tent-pegs strainin' at the weight of taut ropes. Taut ropes, Read.

Mary Sergeant.

Sergeant Carry on.

CORPORAL *on with water.*

Corporal Water, Sergeant.

Mary I'll take it.

SERGEANT *off.*

Corporal Be all right now, Vosquin. Won't be doin' much on that for a couple of weeks. Sit back an' let thy bum-boy minister unto thee.

Jules English pig!

Corporal Belgian ponce.

He goes.

Mary How's the foot?

She goes to look at it.

Jules Get off!

Mary I said I'd look at it for you.

Jules You're always fussing. Like an old woman.

Mary Someone's got to do it.

Jules Why you?

Mary Why not?

Jules You're not qualified.

Mary The surgeon's got a queue a mile long.

Jules You heard what they were saying.

Mary I'll get a dressing.

She prepares what she needs while JULES *removes boot and sock.*

Jules They think we're queer.

Mary Hands off our English privates, Dutchman!

Jules It's not me!

Mary I've seen you, slaverin' over our saddles, nostrils a-quiver, tongue hangin' out.

Jules It's not a joke any more, Mark. I'm losing my self-respect. As a soldier, as a Fleming, as a man. All right, I'm not as good a soldier as you, but people are saying I can't look after myself.

Mary That's nonsense.

Jules I'm not in this war because I like fighting.

Mary You think I am?

Jules No, but it's natural for you. I've seen you before a charge. You wind yourself up. Where others need the heat of battle, you go straight in and kill. I can't do that. I'm in this war because my country's become its battlefield. And if you don't join in, it's fought all over you. I volunteered to share with an Englishman to make for better understanding between our countries.

Mary That's what I wanted too.

Jules But don't you see? What we want means nothing beside the decision of our generals and statesmen. A futile gesture. Perverted by *their* interests. It's unnatural for us to be friends.

Mary Do we stop then?

Jules Mark, I enjoyed riding with you. I was pleased to find we got on. But now it's becoming an obsession. Every party I go on, you come with me. Why are you always hanging round me?

MARY *is standing over him, ready to tend the wound.*

Mary I got a thing about men in uniform.

Jules I'm serious. If things don't change, I'm asking for a transfer.

Pause. MARY *looks at him.*

Mary Lift.

Jules Look at it. Is that a wound to show your grandchildren?

Mary You want children?

Jules Careful. It's through to the bone.

Mary No!

Jules Don't make out you're squeamish. I've seen you cut off worse than toes.

Mary These are your toes.

Jules So?

Mary I'll get some brandy.

She does.

Jules I didn't know you had brandy.

Mary From the Three Horseshoes. In Breda, remember? (*She drinks, hands it to* JULES, *watches his reactions closely as she tends the wound.*) I talked to the landlord. He's selling up. I thought you might be interested when you got out.

Jules It's good stuff.

Mary Officers' issue. I said I had a friend wanted to settle down. Pleasant situation, fresh trout from the river a speciality. A great business.

Jules Why's he selling then?

Mary Can't stand soldiers. Used to be a quiet place. Till the army moved in. Then everyone else moved out.

Jules Why d'you find all this out?

Mary I thought I'd go with you. We could go halves.

Jules Mark, did you hear a word of what I said just now? Two men keeping an army inn together? We'd be a laughing stock!
Mary That wasn't quite how I saw it.
Jules How then? Things are bad enough now!
Mary I am not queer.

Tugs the dressing tight.

Jules Go easy.
Mary Sorry.
Jules Don't tell me men don't interest you.
Mary All right, they do.
Jules I'll get a transfer.
Mary That's it then.

The dressing is complete.

Jules Finished?
Mary Oh no!

Puts a blanket over him.

Jules You like being a nurse, don't you?
Mary What's wrong with that?

Tucks the blanket in.

Jules It makes me helpless. That's right, tuck me in, kiss me goodnight.

MARY *suddenly takes his face and kisses it hard.* JULES *breaks free. She backs off.*

What's the idea!

Struggles out of bedding.

Mary Nothing.
Jules What the hell was that about?

No answer.

What are you, for Christ's sake?

Pause.

Mary Guess.
Jules (*wondering*) Do that again.
Mary No.
Jules You're a woman, aren't you. A fucking woman. Come here.
Mary No.
Jules Shut the tent.
Mary No.
Jules A moment ago you were all over me.

Pause.

What's your name?
Mary Mary.
Jules Mary Read. (*Pause.*) What you doing in the army, for Christ's sake?
Mary Fighting the French, same as you.
Jules What for!
Mary A living.

Pause.

Jules This changes everything. Shut the tent.
Mary No.
Jules I'm cold. I've lost blood.
Mary The blanket.

JULES *pulls the blanket over his legs.*

Jules Get me yours. For my back.
MARY *fetches him a blanket. He grabs her and feels her breasts.*
You are too!
Mary Get off!

She slaps him.

Jules Why'd you do that?
Mary I'm not livestock!
Jules I had to know. How often's a soldier get a woman all to himself? Even
a whore only stays ten minutes.
Mary I'm not flattered.
Jules Come here.
Mary Not on those terms.
Jules Why kiss me then?
Mary You said you'd get a transfer.
Jules No-one even knows you're a woman!
Mary You do.

She goes to a chest.

Jules This is terrible. I can't even walk. You dream about this, Mary.
Mary What d'you think I've done all my life!

Fumbles in the chest.

Jules What are you looking for?
Mary My skirt. I'm going to put it on.
Jules In here?
Mary Turn round.
Jules You can't wear that.
Mary Why not?

Jules In camp?
Mary Just in here. Turn round.

He turns away. She puts the skirt on.

Jules Supposing someone comes by?
Mary You're the man. Get rid of 'em. You can turn round now.
Jules (*turns and looks*) The jacket's wrong.
Mary I haven't got anything else.
Jules Take it off.
Mary No.
Jules What will you do? Go on pretending?
Mary I've told you what I want: The Three Horseshoes.
Jules I don't follow.
Mary For God's sake! How much do I have to humiliate myself!

Pause.

Jules You mean, get married.

Pause.

Five minutes ago I was talking to a man.

Pause.

Give me time.

Pause.

You're not humiliated. The opposite.
Mary Well?
Jules Usually it's men who take the risk.
Mary Men or women, it doesn't matter. We're people. We know each other.
Compared to the rest of it . . .

She gestures desperately, indicating the camp.

Jules Look, shut the tent. I don't want my private life exposed to the entire
battalion.
Mary What private life?
Jules (*smiles*) I haven't had a good screw for weeks.
Mary I haven't had any sort of screw.
Jules I always wondered about that. Well, now's your chance, soldier.

He gets up to shut the tent himself.

Mary Stay there. You've got to rest. I'll get you some tea.
Jules Tea?
Mary I've got to look after you.

She shuts the tent. It gets dark. The SERGEANT comes back.

Sergeant This isn't my normal way. Callin' on a man's tent in the middle of the night is an unfair and delicate business. Night-time's the only time a soldier has to himself. Polishin' accoutrements, sock-darnin', masturbation an' sodomy. Read used to polish his accoutrements. Nowadays I'm not so sure. I did warn him, of course, but my approach should be diplomatic. Pull rank on a soldier off duty, you undermine your authority at other times. Show them you're human, they knuckle under better when it's important to you. Teach you that at Officers' Trainin'. Turned me down on account of poor vocabulary. There's a procedure for this. First a gentle cough. (*He coughs.*) Then tramp about a bit. (*He does.*) Then the call. Private Read!

MARY *appears immediately, still in her skirt.*

Mary Sergeant!

Pause. SERGEANT *looks at her.*

Sergeant Read, I coughed. I gave you time. Surely you could've prepared yourself.

Mary What d'you mean?

Sergeant Your dress, Read.

Mary It's a skirt.

Sergeant I can see that. What's it doing on you?

Mary You'd like it less if it was off me.

Sergeant I thought I made myself clear this afternoon, Read. If anyone less tolerant than myself saw you in that garment, you'd be out on your ear.

Mary That doesn't matter now, Sergeant.

Sergeant I'm a man of the world, Read. Buggery once a month for relief is understandable. But blatant transvestite cohabitation is something else!

Mary There's nothing physical yet, Sergeant.

Sergeant That's even worse. A platonic homosexual relationship in a fighting unit a mile from the French lines! I'd never live it down.

Mary We're getting married.

Sergeant Read, my visit here this evening was originally intended as a friendly admonition in connection with the neglect of your accoutrements. If you choose however to mock the earnest and sacrosanct institution of marriage, I shall have no option but to recommend your immediate discharge.

Mary We're putting in for those tomorrow. We've got our eye on a business. The Three Horseshoes at Breda.

Sergeant That's an army establishment, Read. You can't pursue this kind of liaison in a place like that. You'll be bashed out of your senses.

Mary I'm a woman, Sergeant.

Sergeant I'm beginnin' to think you are.

Mary Really.

She pulls back her coat.

Sergeant Breasts?

MARY *nods.*

I've heard about this sort of thing. Been gettin' common lately. So desperate for recruits, there's no control on quality. I didn't think it could happen to me though. I'll be laughed out of the regiment.

JULES *has come out of the tent.*

Jules Not if you get in first, Sergeant.
Sergeant What d'you mean?
Mary We've got a proposition for you.
Jules We could be in trouble if we don't handle this right. We've got to make a joke of it. Turn the whole thing into a celebration. Regimental party, honourable discharge, officers and men contributing to a whip-round. Just to get us started. Appeal to the officers' sense of humour.
Sergeant Sort of thing they would find funny. Cover the ignominy with a guffaw.
Jules That's right.
Sergeant Don't see it goin' down quite so well in the sergeants' mess.
Mary That's where you come in.
Jules We need your co-operation.
Mary We'd cut you in ten per cent.
Sergeant I'm seein' a completely new side to you, Read. (*To* JULES.) How long've you known?
Mary He found out tonight.
Sergeant I'll be sorry to see you go, Read.
Jules The closer you're connected with this venture, Sergeant, the bigger your prestige.
Sergeant Throwin' yourself away, you realise, on a Dutchman.
Mary We break the news tomorrow afternoon. If you take Jules' hat, you can start the ball rolling.
Sergeant Well, I don't know.
Mary Take it anyway. He doesn't need it any more.

Gives him the hat.

Sergeant (*thoughtful*) Thankyou.
Mary Goodnight, Sergeant.

She and JULES *go back into the tent.*

Sergeant Goodnight, Read.

Pauses in thought a moment, then goes.

The SINGERS *come on and sing:*

Singers So it's goodnight to the sergeant
             and goodbye to the army.

The child made a prisoner
    in growing up grows free.
She puts right the wrong done to her
    the mould she was cast in,
And steps out now a woman
    a human being.

But does a drop in the ocean
    change the colour of the water?
When the inner landscape brightens
    does the world outside alter?
Across the whole map of the West
    England's canopy's still spread.
Others fight the same oppression
    with a different kind of dread.

For the Cormacs came to Charleston
    And soon Peg Brennan died.
It was Ann who had to keep the house
    though she never could keep inside.
She loved hunting and fishing and shooting
    with Charley, her Indian friend.
And the beaux of Carolina
    found her hard to get in the end.

They announce . . .

1716 CHARLESTON, CAROLINA

. . . and go off.

ANN, *sitting by a river, fishing.* FORTESQUE KENDAL *approaches her.*

Kendal Ann Cormac?

No answer.

Fishing, I see.

No answer.

You're not asleep, are you?

ANN *turns slowly.*

Name of Kendal. Fortesque Kendal. We're neighbours. Mind if I sit with you?

As he lowers himself ANN *gets up swiftly and gets him in a half-nelson.*

Ann Did I say you could sit with me?

Kendal No.

Ann Why do it then?

Kendal We're neighbours. I thought we might get acquainted.

Ann You haven't heard I always make the first move?

Kendal Pardon?

Ann Sexually.

Kendal No I hadn't. Heard.

Ann You've been frequenting the wrong circles, the *gentle* circles. If I want a man to get acquainted with me, I let him know. *I* get acquainted with *him*. I don't simper in corners, I don't powder my nose in a mirror, and I don't lower my fan. That way you only get stuffed shirts. The men I want I let know.

She releases him.

Kendal I see.

Ann You're a gentleman, aren't you. I can always tell gentlemen by the way they operate. They sort of creep up. I don't like it. I can see it coming a mile off. Smugglers I like. And pirates. If a pirate wants you, he says so. If he doesn't, he leaves you alone. Pirates don't mess about.

Pause.

Kendal We have the next plantation, you know. That side.

Ann I wondered when you'd be round. I've had the other side over already.

Kendal Terence? Oh, how did you get on?

Ann You thought I'd be an easy lay, didn't you.

Kendal Sorry?

Ann Just because I go with pirates, every gentleman in Charleston thinks I'm an easy lay. That's the way their minds work. Didn't you know I slept with pirates?

Kendal No.

Ann Don't lie, it's all over Charleston.

Kendal Honestly. I don't get around much.

Ann I'm not surprised. D'you fancy me then?

Kendal Sorry?

Ann Reckon me, do you?

Kendal I don't know.

Ann Come on! Yes or no.

Kendal Well, yes.

Ann Try it on then.

Kendal Here?

Ann What's wrong with here?

Kendal Well . . . well, nothing.

Ann I warn you, if you try it on, you'll have your work cut out.

Kendal Why?

Ann I'll fight you.

Kendal Why!

Ann If you got me pregnant, you'd have to marry me.

Kendal Of course I would. But I don't understand.

Ann If you laid me, and I got pregnant, we'd be married, and your plantation and ours would be joined in your name, and we'd be a rich and respected couple. That's the way it works in Charleston, right? D'you fancy that?

Kendal I could think of worse.

Ann Want to try it on with the Cormac plantation then?

Kendal I don't know.

Ann Think.

Kendal All right.

Ann It's on?

Kendal Yes.

Ann Try it then.

> KENDAL *grabs for her clumsily straight away.* ANN *slips away easily.*

Cormac versus Kendal. I'll call my Indian.

Kendal Your Indian?

Ann Half Yamassee, half negro. Best of both worlds. He sees all my fights.

> *Goes to whistle.*

Kendal Your fights?

Ann You call them conquests, don't you?

Kendal Is it quite proper for a slave to watch?

Ann Don't be so stuffy! (*Whistles.*) Now think what you're doing. It won't be easy, I fight hard. You can't blunder in like you did just now.

Kendal I wasn't expecting that kind of resistance.

Ann I warned you. You've got to be clever.

> CHARLEY, *the Indian, appears.*

He's going to rape me, Charley.

Kendal Does he have to watch?

Ann I value his criticism. He taught me all I know.

Charley You better no try, mister.

Ann He's a gentleman, Charley.

Charley You better no try.

Kendal Really!

> *He flies at* ANN. *She dodges and gets him in a hold, slams it on hard then releases it, hits him hard in the stomach and face.* KENDAL *totters and sits down.*

Ann They never believe me, Charley.

> CHARLEY *laughs.*

Had enough?

Kendal I don't know what my father's going to say.
Ann Tell him you tried to rape Ann Cormac. Then, like the rest of Charleston,
he'll believe you.

> KENDAL *dives for* ANN's *legs. A fierce struggle ensues in which* KENDAL
> *gives his best, but* ANN's *ferocity is too much for him. Finally she gains the*
> *upper hand.*

Ann Give in?
Kendal No!
Ann Give in?
Kendal Uch.

> *She lets him go.*

Kendal I give in.
Ann (*slapping him*) I don't allow giving in!
Charley You start, now you finish.
Ann (*slapping him again*) Come on!
Kendal I tell you, I give in! You're the winner!
Ann You tried to steal my honour. I'm going to kill you.
Kendal No!

> *He tries to run away.* CHARLEY *stops him.*

Charley You stay. You fight.
Kendal No!

> ANN *comes up and hits him.*

No, please!
Ann What's the matter with you? I gave you your chance. You said you'd
fight, so fight!
Kendal (*almost screaming*) No!

> ANN *hits him several times. Yelling and sobbing,* KENDAL *falls to the ground.*
> WILL CORMAC *comes on, drawn by the noise.*

Ann They're not like Indians, Charley. They don't know commitment.
Will My God, Ann, is this another young gentleman you've been clubbing
within an inch of his life?
Ann I'm getting fed up with it.
Will This is the third time in as many weeks. That's no behaviour for a
planter's daugher. You're heiress to a sizeable fortune now, which I've
built from nothing. You should be marrying into the Carolina aristoc-
racy, not carrying on like a twelve-year-old tomboy.
Ann They try it on.
Will You lead them on.
Ann It's the season for it.
Will You're a terrible liar, Ann.

Ann I am not. Substantially.

Will Ann, I find it difficult to believe so many young gentlemen are prepared to lay down their consciousness for the dubious pleasure of overpowering you.

Ann I warned him!

Will I'm surprised they're not wise to you yet.

Ann They want the prize: our rice. Carolina Gold! If they want it, they've got to fight for it. I'm not being parcelled off to some anaemic dummy.

Will All right, let's go in.

Ann Who are you talking to?

Will You. We're going in.

Ann I'm staying here. I'm meeting someone.

Will Who?

Ann James Bonney.

Will In one breath you talk of anaemic dummies, the next you tie yourself up with the very article. The man's a smuggler, Ann.

Ann A businessman, father. Like you.

Will There's no comparison.

Ann No comparison! Are you pretending now that all our rice which by law should go through London actually goes there?

Will (*eyeing* KENDAL *anxiously*) This is not the place to discuss this, Ann.

Ann Are you pretending our trade with grasping Europe brings more profit than selling on the sly to the pirate islands?

Will It's natural the mother country should seek to prosper from its colonies. But they'd think little of us if we didn't show some independence.

Ann England isn't your mother country. You're an Irishman! You're talking like a snot-nosed Pinckney, or one of those damned Ashley Coopers.

Will This is a new country, Ann. We're all equal. We all have the chance to better ourselves.

Ann If we're all equal, where are we bettering to?

Will Certainly not to James Bonney. A more sickly and shifty-eyed party I have yet to see.

Ann He's deceptive.

Will Certainly he's deceived every servant girl from here to Jamestown. And you too, if you see what they see.

Ann He's ambitious, got a head for money. A smuggler who aspires to be a gentleman. The only sort of man you and I could ever agree on, Father.

Will He's an idle waster with nothing on his mind but my money.

Ann Got all I need on him.

Will You're a foolish girl to mix with these people, Ann. They'd murder you for your eyebrows if they could find a market for them.

Ann I've seen planters murder for a bucket of rice. I won't be used!

Will Now come on, pick up that fellow and let's get inside.

Ann He's not hurt. It's only the shock of it.

Will He needs treatment.

Ann Why should I give him the hurts in the first place, if only to see them mended after? You don't build a wall to knock it down again.

Will It's not polite, Ann. Now inside.

Ann I'm meeting James!

Will I'll have nothing to do with James Bonney. He's a deserter and a smuggler, and he'll get no money of mine!

Ann Your money, that's all this is about really. Listen, my mother worked herself to death for *your* money, and since she died, it's been me. I've cooked, hunted, even traded for you. I've slaved for you, like Charley and the blacks in the fields. But I've learned to look after myself too. And if you're so ungrateful now, not to let me decide about what I've earned, I'll go where I'm valued.

Will Inside.

Ann You take him.

Pause. Battle of will which ANN *wins.* CORMAC *helps* KENDAL *to his feet.*

Will Can you walk?

Kendal I seem to have chosen a bad time.

Will I'll give you my arm. Charley, help me.

The two of them help KENDAL *off.*

Ann My Indian's not your slave! I freed him, I pay him! – Mind the gentleman doesn't touch you up, Charley!

Will I'll have nothing to do with James Bonney!

The three go. JAMES BONNEY *comes out of hiding.*

Bonney Doesn't like me, does he?

Ann James! Why didn't you show yourself?

Bonney It would've been hours before we got rid of him. I haven't got much time.

Ann Why, what's the news?

Bonney A boat for New Providence tomorrow morning.

Ann And we're taking it?

Bonney Depends if he'll give you enough.

Ann What he won't give I'll take.

Bonney I'm a dealer, Ann. Are you a bargain or not?

Ann You're a smuggler, James. Even without a dowry I'm better cargo than a tavern tart.

Bonney Prove it.

Ann Help yourself.

She stands, legs apart, inviting and challenging.

Bonney I'll meet you tomorrow morning. On the quay at five.

Ann You're on.

They go off in opposite directions. The SINGERS *come on and sing:*

Singers So it's goodbye to Daddy
 and goodbye to the plantation.
The child is deviating
 from the nation's deviation.
She puts right the wrong done to her
 the mould she was cast in,
And steps out now a woman,
 a human being.

So escaping from is fun,
 but where to and what for?
You can't live alone
 and other people are the law.
And while Charleston's other people
 make a tomboy break free,
In Holland other people
 end a wife's liberty.

They announce . . .

1718 BREDA IN HOLLAND. THE THREE HORSESHOES

. . . and go off.

A table with two chairs stacked on it. Another table on which JULES VOSQUIN's *corpse is laid out. A third table with a knapsack, which* MARY *is packing.* ELIZABETH, *a serving girl at the inn, comes in and watches her.*

Elizabeth Are we not opening today, Mrs Vosquin?

Mary No, Elizabeth.

Elizabeth You're definitely leaving then.

Mary I've laid Jules out. They're coming to bury him this afternoon. I'll go first thing tomorrow.

Elizabeth Who'll look after the inn?

Mary I haven't been able to sell it, Elizabeth. After what happened no-one will buy. There's no work for you here, I'm afraid. You'll have to go back to your parents.

Elizabeth He was a good man, Mrs Vosquin. A good man to work for.

MARY *stops packing, leans on the table. Her head sinks.*

I'm sorry. I shouldn't have said . . .

Pause.

Don't go, Mrs Vosquin.

Mary Six years I've been here, Elizabeth. The best of my life. Before I even asked the question, that man knew the answer.

Elizabeth It shouldn't have happened, Mrs Vosquin. Really. It wasn't fair. You must stay.

Mary They call it peace. Prosperity for Europe. But for who? Even before the cease-fire English troops came through here, deserting their foreign comrades, drunk and ashamed because their generals were carving up Europe with the France that had been our common enemy. Then they went home. With nothing to do, no discipline, they lived off the land. Thieved and murdered. The Three Horseshoes lost business, the Dutch spat on our English soldiers. People refused to talk to my husband. Because he married an Englishwoman. And it *was* shameful, Elizabeth, what my country did. But he never made it an issue in this house. Then Dutch soldiers find an inn with a master as gentle and generous as any man alive. They drink together, swop stories, and because he married an Englishwoman – or perhaps because they couldn't pay – they take him outside after we've all gone to bed. They beat his body raw, kick his bones to splinters, cut the hair from his head and carve pieces from him like a liver. Then they leave the carcass on the doorstep. My husband, Elizabeth. Prosperity for who?

Elizabeth I don't know, Mrs V. I don't understand anything any more.

Mary I've lost a husband and you've lost a job, that's all there is to understand. If they can do that to a man, what chance does a woman stand, now they've let loose the fire in the soldiers' bellies? If I stay now, I'll finish up like him. Battered and flattened like this whole continent. What's left is alive with maggots and fit only for the vultures in London and Paris. (*Hands* ELIZABETH *her trousers.*) Take these upstairs. I'm wearing them tomorrow.

Elizabeth These are trousers, Ma'am.

Mary And these.

She hands ELIZABETH *her boots.*

ELIZABETH *doesn't understand.*

I'm going back to what I know, that's all. I can handle a sword as well as them. If England's revolution can only suck Europe dry, I'll go where the juice is they fight over. Where they suck their blood from. I'll sign on a ship to the New World. This place is dead.

Elizabeth What shall I do?

Mary Don't marry a soldier.

They go off. The SINGERS *come on and begin the song. As they do, they are joined by characters from the next scene.*

Singers Damn, damn the English to hell,
Their army, their navy, their King as well.
For they've sucked the world dry from bottom to top
And left us poor beggars not even a drop.

Damn, damn the English to hell,
The French and the Dutch and the Spanish as well.

For they're all just as bad, the Portuguese too.
Get rid of the lot, so there's just left we few.

Damn, damn the English to hell,
But then while you're at it, damn us all as well.
For we're English too though we blush at the name,
And their shame is ours for we play the same game.

Damn, damn the English to hell,
Their army, their navy, their King as well.
For they've sucked the world dry from bottom to top
And left us poor beggars not even a drop.

The SINGERS *announce . . .*

1720 PIERRE'S CAFE. 'THE HOUSE OF LORDS' IN NEW PROVIDENCE

. . . and go off.

Four tables, eight chairs. A rough, small, proscenium stage with curtains drawn. THOMAS EARL *and* JOHN DAVIES, *pirates, sit arm-in-arm at one table. An* OLD WHORE *and* THOMAS SPENLOW, *drinking quietly on his own, sit separately at two next to each other.* JOHN HOWELL *sits at the fourth.* PIERRE *gets up on the stage.*

Pierre Bonsoir, mesdames et messieurs! Welcome to Pierre's 'Ouse of Lords, ze most notorious and most outrageous café en New Providence!
Davies An' the most expensive!

Ironic cheers and whistles from onlookers.

Pierre A small price, messieurs, for ze last taste of liberty in ze West Indies.
Davies Don' kid yerself!
Pierre Messieurs, mesdames, zere are cynics 'oo say ze hey-day of piracy is over.
Howell An' it is!

Boos and hisses from onlookers.

Pierre But 'ere at Pierre's 'Ouse of Lords – unlike ze other établissement of ze same name – zose 'oo farm ze island's riches can also enjoy zeir 'arvest. Ze best food, ze best drink, ze best women, ze best men . . .
Earl French fairy!
Old Whore You can talk, lover.
Davies Us? We work for our livin'. An' 'ard. All you women do is the enjoyin'.
Old Whore Enjoyin' you *is* hard work, lover.
Howell Get on with it!
Pierre Merci, monsieur. Eh bien, as you all know well, you can also enjoy at Pierre's ze best entertainment.

Howell If you shut up we might!
Old Whore 'E says the same thing every night.
Howell Tell us somethin' we don' know, Pierre!

ANN *comes on.*

Pierre That would not be difficile, mon ami. – Alors, maintenant, especially for your délectation, we present tonight une pièce dramatique.

Pause.

A play.
Earl Oh no!
Old Whore Not again!

Groans and boos from onlookers.

Pierre English Philistines!
Davies Alien snob!
Pierre Performed, mesdames et messieurs, by our good friend Stroller . . .
Old Whore Not 'im again!
Davies Whyn't yer get some decent acts, Pierre?
Old Whore Got more sense'n t' stay on this poxy island, that's why.
Pierre . . . Stroller an' ze crew of zat famous an' much-loved sea-artist Captain 'Calico' Jack Rackham!
Davies Good ol' Jack!

Wild cheers and whistles from onlookers.

Pierre A play entitled . . . un moment.

He puts his head behind the curtain.

Old Whore 'E's forgotten it!
Davies Wake up, Pierre, it's nearly bed-time.
Pierre (*loud whisper*) Stroller, comment s'appelle-t-elle, la pièce?
Stroller (*same*) Eh?
Pierre (*same*) O mais le titre alors! Ze title!
Stroller Oh. 'The Governor.'
Pierre Voilà. (*Turns to onlookers again.*) Mesdames et messieurs, we present 'Ze Governor'!

PIERRE *climbs down from the stage. Pause. The curtain moves.*

Stroller (*behind curtain, loud whisper*) Come on, what's the matter with you?
Blackie (*same*) It's come out again.
Stroller (*same*) For Christ's sake!
Davies 'Aving trouble with yer fly, Blackie!
Howell Come on, Stroller, let's be 'avin' yer!
Stroller It's not me, it's Blackie, 'E's got stage-fright.
Blackie I ain'!

Stroller (*comes through curtain*) 'E's got these lighted tapers in 'is 'at, see, cos 'e's playin' Blackbeard. Only they keep fallin' out.

Earl What's 'e wan' tapers for?

Stroller 'E's got t' look the part.

Davies Why? If 'e says 'e's Blackbeard, we'll believe 'im.

Blackie (*coming out*) They keep catchin' me 'air alight.

Howell We remember what the ol' bastard looked like.

Old Whore Some of us is tryin' t' forget.

Howell You don' 'ave t' do it all for us.

Blackie I got a look right.

Stroller Come on!

Takes BLACKIE *back behind curtain.*

Howell Stupid pillock. Sees 'isself as Blackbeard's reincarnation. Carryin' the torch so the memory lives on.

Ann What good's the memory when the possibility's gone?

Davies 'Ello! *Mrs* Rackham in tonight, too?

Ann I'm no-one's missis.

Davies So we 'eard.

Earl Mrs Bonney gave Mr Bonney the elbow.

Ann I was never anyone's missis.

Davies No-one's an' anyone's!

Laughter amongst the men. PIERRE *gets back on the stage.*

Pierre But Madame is right, mes amis! Ze possibility of a free life 'as gone. An' Stroller's play is about just zis. If you listened, you might learn somezing.

Davies From Stroller! (*Laughs.*)

Pierre 'Ave we not 'ad for ze past year a Governor on ze island, like Governor Lawes in Jamaica, sent by ze English to claim it for zeir own?

Earl Quite right too! Englan' for ever!

Ann Quite right, he's systematically destroying the way of life we built up here?

Earl Woodes Rogers is all right. Used to be a privateer 'imself.

Ann A privateer isn't a pirate, Tom. Woodes Rogers was a privateer when Spain controlled trade in the islands. Now England does, she calls her privateers pirates.

Earl Woodes Rogers is all right. He knows our ways.

Ann That's what makes him dangerous. He's changing our ways to suit the government in London.

Davies Don' matter what they call us. We are what we always were: sea-artists.

Ann Not now they're making farmers of you. Generously allowing you twenty square yards of the land *you* pioneered.

Pierre In exchange for which you 'ave to be good boys.

Ann That's why Calico Jack and me are leaving the island. We want to get a crew together.

Pierre Leaving? Mais chérie, don't be so boring. Ze only way to enjoy trouble is to fight it.

Ann We can't fight this, it's gone too far. My husband and his friend Turnley, have gone and filed a complaint against me. For going with Jack while I'm still officially married. So now Woodes Rogers has threatened me with a public whipping.

YOUNG WHORE *wanders on and sits with* SPENLOW.

Pierre But you divorced zis Bonney!

Ann We left each other. All he ever wanted was my father's money. And the kind of column I was after wasn't made of pounds, shillings and pence.

Laughter from the others.

Pierre But Jack paid him, non?

Ann The English don't recognise divorce by sale.

Howell (*comes over to* ANN) No-one's an' anyone's is right.

Old Whore Leave 'er alone. – Wan' a watch that one, Ann.

Ann And to think I ran away with Bonney 'cos I thought he had more go than the stuffed shirts in Charleston. Look at him now. Turtle-fishing and spying for the Governor!

Pierre Forget him, Ann. Enjoy yourself!

Ann This is urgent, Pierre. I've got to have a serious talk with these men.

Pierre Let zem 'ave zeir fun first, hein? You can talk to zem later. – More drinks!

Takes an order from SPENLOW.

Ann All he thinks about's his business.

Howell Never mind, sweetheart, I'll be serious.

Ann Piss off. I'm sitting with the ladies.

Old Whore That's right, dear, over here. I got somethin' t' show you.

Takes a jar out of her bag.

Ann What's that?

Old Whore Remedy for clap. Indian girl give it me. Been usin' it years on the islands.

Ann Let's see.

Takes the jar.

Young Whore 'Ow much yer give for it?

Old Whore Crown.

Young Whore You been done. That's yam cream.

Old Whore Yam cream!

Young Whore Put it on yer tits, stops 'em saggin'. For a night.

Howell What you need, bag!

Ann Shut your noise.

Old Whore What about the clap?

Young Whore You ain't got it, so why worry?

Howell Believe that a week after!

Old Whore Use yer 'and, it's safer.

Young Whore Good stuff though. Takes the muck out yer skin.

Old Whore 'Ave it on toast if it's yams.

Young Whore Why not? It's not poison. (*Scoops some out and tries it.*) Eurgh. Got somethin' else in.

Ann You're quiet, Tom.

Spenlow Tryin' a 'ear meself think.

Howell Your sparklin' conversation's struck 'im dumb.

Young Whore Shut up, 'e's lovely. Buyin' me drinks an' don' wan' nothin', 'e says.

Howell (*comes over to* ANN *and the others*) Cos 'e's not a man. Just like Mr Bonney an' the others.

Ann And you are, I suppose.

Howell Even your Jack Rackham's all show. Now when you look at me, you're lookin' at a real pirate.

Ann The real ones all left the island. What's left are all creeping up Woodes Rogers' arsehole.

Howell Not me!

Ann I've seen you, outside his office. Queueing for your lousy twenty square yards.

Howell I got t' do somethin'! I'm broke.

Ann Make a bit then. Get yourself a ship.

Howell Whose? Spenlow's?

Spenlow All right by me.

Ann I'm glad to hear that, Tom.

Spenlow It ain' mine anyway. None of us is workin' for ourselves now. Same everywhere. In Jamaica you work for Governor Lawes or Provost Forbes. Here you work for Woodes Rogers. Like your husban'.

Ann And this one. (*Referring to* HOWELL.)

Howell Don' mention me in the same breath as James Bonney. Woodes Rogers would never have got in if Bonney hadn't piloted him past the round rocks.

Young Whore Saved 'is bottom from the King's Bollocks, did 'e!

The WHORES *laugh.*

Ann Never mind the King's. Now there's a Governor in, have you got the balls to get out?

Howell Show you if yer like.
Ann I'm sorry I spoke.
Howell What can you do? There's no-one goin' out now.
Ann Jack and me are. In Spenlow's boat.
Spenlow What else is new?
Ann We've only moved it round the coast.
Spenlow Only!
Ann You said you didn't care.
Spenlow Just a manner of speakin'.
Ann D'you care enough to fight for it?
Spenlow (*defeated*) That's all I need.
Ann (*to the others*) We'll take any man with us who's willing.
Howell Calico Jack's takin' a woman on board?
Old Whore She's takin' him!
Howell The old days really are over.
Ann Well?
Howell I'll go if you give me a kiss.
Ann What's your name?
Howell John Howell.
Ann You're on, John Howell.

> *She grabs him and kisses him violently. The* WHORES *laugh as he struggles.* JAMES BONNEY, ALEXANDER FORBES *and* CAPTAIN BARNET *come on.* SPENLOW *sees them coming.*

Spenlow Oh Christ.

> *He slips off.*

Ann What's the matter?
Young Whore Somethin' the cat's brought in.
Ann (*seeing them, to* BONNEY) What do you want?
Bonney A drink.
Ann Why *here* all of a sudden?
Bonney Business more than pleasure.
Ann Spying on me, are you?
Bonney May I introduce Alexander Forbes, Provost Marshal of Jamaica and a planter whose connection with these islands goes back many years. And Captain Barnet, Commander of the King's Fleet.
Ann Funny company you're keeping now.
Barnet Shut up!
Old Whore Oh, like that, is it.
Forbes We lost a boat this afternoon. I'm looking for its captain.
Howell What's his name?
Forbes Thomas Spenlow. I believe he sometimes drinks here.
Howell I haven't seen 'im today, though. – Have you?

Davies No.

Others murmur 'no', shake their heads.

Earl Probably out lookin' for your boat, Mr Forbes.

Forbes I mention this because there's also a rumour, Mistress Bonney, that you're thinking of running off with this Rackham fellow you've been forbidden to see. Evading the Governor's justice.

Old Whore Call that justice?

Bonney Shut your noise, whore. This is none of your business.

Old Whore You're right. Men are my business, an' you ain' one.

Young Whore Yeh, Pierre's more a man than you are.

Pierre Merci pour rien.

Barnet A word of warning to you all. Provost Forbes and myself are here to discuss with the Governor ways of stamping out the pirate menace for good. From now on this establishment will be under close surveillance.

Old Whore Arsehole.

Barnet We could have it shut now for what we've seen and heard.

Young Whore Piss off.

Pierre (*to* BARNET) When scum like you can do zat, monsieur, Providence will be no place for Pierre.

Forbes I'm glad to hear it, sir.

Pierre And now please, you go. I don't serve informers.

All the pirates are watching the three closely.

Bonney (*to* ANN) Got a ship?

Ann Find out.

Pierre No more questions, gentlemen.

He comes forward to face them squarely. BARNET *reaches for his sword. One or two of the pirates stand.*

It's bad for business.

Bonney All right.

He turns and goes with FORBES *and* BARNET.

Young Whore Ha! Couldn't get it up in his sleep, that one!

Ann Turtle fisher!

Old Whore Couldn't catch one if it was lyin' on its back.

Pierre But ze others with him, zey are dangerous.

Spenlow (*coming back*) They gone?

Davies What's the matter, Tom? 'Fraid of a bit of gold braid?

Spenlow (*to* ANN) You've landed me right in it. That boat belongs to Forbes' brother-in-law.

Howell The one 'ose connections go right back?

Spenlow An' there was Bonney askin' if you got a boat!

They all laugh.

Pierre A drink on ze 'ouse to celebrate!

He goes off.

STROLLER *comes through the curtain.*

Stroller You ready now?
Earl You just missed the fun, Stroller.
Stroller What fun?
Old Whore Never mind! Get your bloody thing over, so we can drink in peace!
Stroller Ladies an' gentlemen, we present 'The Governor'!

On the stage the curtain draws back on the tableau of BLACKIE *as Blackbeard with sulphurous tapers burning under his hat, and* NOAH HARWOOD *as Captain Sam Bellamy, both in exaggerated theatrical poses.* BLACKIE *fires two pistol shots in the air. Appreciative reaction from onlookers.*

Earl Go it, Blackie boy!

STROLLER *walks on as 'Governor Jack'.*

Stroller Captain Teach, there can be no bargain between the Governor of one of His Majesty's Colonies and pirates like yourself and Captain Bellamy.
Harwood Sea-artists is what we are, sir, sea-artists!
Earl That's Noah. Noah Harwood!
Ann (*to* HOWELL) He does Bellamy good. Watch this.
Harwood That French ship in your harbour, sir, is laden with sixty barrels of sugar. Her entire load is yours if ye sign the ship over to us legal.
Stroller But you stole her, Captain Bellamy. You and Captain Teach sunk her escort and tipped her crew into a longboat.
Harwood We needn't have, sir, if her captain hadn't insulted my men. I remonstrated with him. He had only himself to blame.
Davies That's right, Noah, you tell 'im!
Harwood 'Damn my beard,' I said. 'I'm sorry the men won't let ye have your sloop back, for she might've been of use to ye, and I scorn to do anyone mischief when it's not to my advantage. But damn the sloop, we must sink her!'

Cheers from onlookers.

Stroller The facts however remain, Captain Bellamy. You sailed into our harbour, bombarded us for three days, then ordered us to hand over a chest of medicine worth three hundred pounds for your wounded.
Blackie We did that so ye'd know what kind of men you're dealing with!
Stroller A letter would have sufficed.
Blackie Damn ye, sir? Damn this prevarication!

He fires another pistol.

Earl Whoa-hey!

Davies Go it, Blackie boy!

Harwood Well, sir? Do we have her or not?

Stroller That ship is stolen, gentlemen. Ye're asking me to be your accomplice.

Harwood But ye've traded with us before, Governor Jack. Why should ye be so scupulous now?

Stroller The trade we did in the past, Captain Bellamy, was legitimate.

Incredulous hoots and whistles from onlookers.

Earl Shoot the bugger, Blackie!

Harwood But ye knew what we sold ye in the past was stolen, Governor. How else would poor sea-orphans like ourselves come by such cargoes?

Stroller That was for you to say, Captain, and me to trust. My honour as a gentleman would forbid me to do business with thieves.

Blackie Damn yer honour! It's never stopped ye afore!

Stroller Gentlemen, only today I received strict instructions from the Admiralty to stop piratical trade in this town.

Blackie The answer to this mystery, Governor Jack, is ye're a damn crafty knave as only believes what he wants to!

Cheers from onlookers.

Harwood Damn ye, sir, ye're a sneaking puppy! And so are all men who submit to laws made by rich men for their own security. There is only this difference between us: they rob the poor under the cover of the law, while we plunder the rich under the protection of nothing but our own courage. I am a free prince and have as much right to make war on the whole world as he who has a hundred ships at sea and an army of 100,000 in the field.

Huge, wild applause from onlookers. BLACKIE *fires another pistol.*

Stroller Gentlemen, to repay your wrongs, I suggest you turn the ship's cargo over to me – on behalf of the town. I will declare the ship herself leaky, liable to sink and block the harbour. Then you can take her out and burn her. In this way no trace of your guilt will remain, and you will be free men.

Blackie Hell's breath, Governor Jack, that's no favour ye're doing us.

Harwood Ye're taking the cargo we worked for and saving yer own neck into the bargain.

Blackie We get nothing save the pleasure of burning her!

Stroller Then I'm afraid I shall be forced to bring criminal proceedings against you.

Blackie God's blood! I'll kill the villain! I'll run him through!

He draws his sword. Shouts from the audience.

Earl Go on, Blackie, do for 'im!
Davies Finish 'im off!

STROLLER *takes out a pistol.*

Earl Watch out, he's got a pistol!
Howell Hold on, we're comin'!

EARL, DAVIES *and* HOWELL *get up and advance on the stage. A table is turned over.* EARL *fires his pistol at* STROLLER.

Harwood What's goin on?

He can't see against the footlights.

Stroller They're bloody shootin' at us!
Blackie Bastards!

Shoots back blindly.

Earl (*charging the stage*) Yaa-aa!
Stroller Gentlemen, gentlemen, why this discord? It's only a play. And the moral is, we must stick together!
Davies Get 'im!

With a yell DAVIES, EARL *and* HOWELL *climb on the stage.* EARL *jumps on* STROLLER'*s back.* HARWOOD *goes to* STROLLER'*s aid, then all five pitch in. The* WHORES *pelt the stage with whatever's handy.* ANN *laughs.* PIERRE *flaps.*

Pierre Messieurs, messieurs! Mais qu'est-ce que vous faites alors? Vous m'apportez la ruine! O mais, ça alors!

Over the riot STROLLER *struggles free and says his piece.*

Stroller We could build an empire here if we pulled together. Rome itself was started by sheep thieves and runaway slaves. Force is the key, and force we have. If we took the Indians, the labourers and settlers under our wing, we could make slaves of those who don't recognise our sovereignty. Declare ourselves a legal monarchy and every court in Europe would recognise us. They'd even send ambassadors!
Harwood Good! We'll make you Prime Minister!

RACKHAM *comes on with* GEORGE FETHERSTONE *and* MARY.

Rackham WHAT THE FUCK'S GOIN' ON!

They stop, turn and look.

Pierre Ah Jack, mon ami. Comme je suis heureux de te voir!
Rackham Noah, I left you in charge. What the hell happened?
Harwood Well, Jack, we were doin' this sort of play thing with Stroller an', like, it got a bit out of hand.

Rackham (*to* ANN) You were supposed to get these blokes together.

Ann I got one man: John Howell.

Rackham Pleased t' meet you, John. That's all we got too. George an' me's been over the whole island. Only one man who's not turned farmer or turtler – Mark Read. Ann Bonney.

Mary (*shaking hands*) Pleased t' meet you.

Ann Why you coming, Mark?

Mary I want to get off New Providence.

Old whore Don' we all, dear.

Stroller Stay together! Stay an' fight! It's the only way!

Fetherstone Shut yer mouth.

Ann Pirate, are you?

Mary I was forced.

Ann You can fight though?

Fetherstone 'E was a soldier four years. In Flanders.

Ann What does that prove?

Fetherstone Uses that sword like a third arm.

Ann What about his third leg?

Rackham 'E'll keep it between 'is other two. Like everyone else on this trip. – We got a boat.

Ann Tom's.

Spenlow 'Ere, 'ang on!

Rackham Time you took a rest, Tom. (*Puts money on* SPENLOW'*s table.*) So you can buy a round for a change. – Right then, 'oo's interested?

Noah Where you goin'?

Rackham First stop: 'er 'usband's friend, Turnley. 'E's turtlin' off the Caymans. With any luck we'll 'ave 'is bollocks for Sunday breakfast.

Noah Is this a proper trip, Jack? Or just revenge for you two?

Rackham There's still places left for free men in these islands, Noah. Cuba, Hispaniola. The wealth's there. An' it's our right to enjoy its takin'.

Earl We'd 'elp you fight 'ere if you stayed on.

Rackham What for? A piece of land you can't dance a jig on?

Noah It's all we're left with, Jack. Everywhere else is owned. Land gives you substance. If we don' get some, we're nothin'.

Rackham The whole of the western seas is ours by right. If we want it, we can get it. What's to stop us?

Mary Governor Lawes an' the English Navy for a start.

Rackham Even in Jamaica they don' like payin' t' keep English forces on the island. Port Royal's wide open. We could live off the pickin's there an' retire in luxury before they caught us.

Davies If we're runnin' the ship as equals like we used to, Jack, I'm happy.

Earl An' me.

Harwood Fair shares an' compensation for injury?

Rackham Of course.

Harwood I'm in then.

Blackie Me an' all.

Rackham Get that muck off you then, an' let's go.

Blackie Yahoo!

Pierre Jack! A drink before you go.

Rackham No time, Pierre.

Pierre But you pay for zeirs, yes?

Rackham 'Ere. (*Gives* PIERRE *money*.) Keep a roun' standin' for when we come back rich men.

Stroller If you stood still a moment, Jack Rackham, you'd see the mistake you're makin'. The old days are over. An' you're runnin' away from the last chance they're givin' you. Cut yourself off now, you do it for ever.

Rackham Stroller, you're a pain.

Ann If we stood as still as you, Stroller, we'd do nothing at all.

They go. The SINGERS *come on and sing:*

Singers   So they're pushed to extremes
        on the map's furthest edge.
    The victims come together
        to take their last revenge.
    A desperate rearguard action,
        a last defensive ploy,
    Against a growing Empire
        they preserve their dwindling joy.

    For it takes two to seal a bargain
        and make this world go round.
    And if the deal's not good enough
        a new one will be found.
    But though to the mainland now
        they seem a bird of prey,
    The bird remains dependent
        even when it's flown away.

    For now within the crew itself
        appears a contradiction:
    Two extraordinary women
        double victims amongst victims.
    And though we've seen from the outside
        how these problems have evolved,
    The question now inside the crew is
        how will they be solved?

They go off.

ACT II

In front of the map there is now the rigging of a ship. Ropes, capstan, ship's wheel, a hatch.

The SINGERS *come on and sing:*

Singers   Cast off from the mainland now
           and outside the law.
       But needing to feed upon
           the Empire even more,
       A group of England's malcontents
           run their own lives.
       Consent the only rule by which
           they organise.

       But in this male community
           two women have arrived.
       They're special cases, and for them
           the customs don't provide.
       One makes herself exceptional
           the other will abide.
       But now the crew face problems
           both in – and outside.

      They announce . . .

FEBRUARY, 1720   ABOARD RACKHAM'S SHIP OFF THE CAYMANS

     . . . and go off. MARY *comes on, followed soon by* RACKHAM.

Rackham Where you goin', Read?

Mary Rackham?

Rackham Right first time. What you doin' on deck?

Mary I was off to the Heads.

Rackham This time of night?

Mary I got funny bowels.

Rackham I been watchin' you, Read. You're always sneakin' off, always on your own. Three weeks at sea an' I never seen you take a dip with the others. You ought to stink like a barrel of seaweed. What's your secret?

Mary I get by.

     Pause. RACKHAM *lights a pipe.*

Rackham Never found Turnley, did we.

Mary No.

Rackham Symbolic mission of revenge t' kick us off, an' it failed.

Mary We were unlucky, that's all.

Rackham Not unlucky. We tracked him down systematically. We found his crew, six turtles on their backs an' a hog ready pickled. We even found his ship. Why weren't he on it?

Mary I don't know.

Pause. RACKHAM *looks at her, smokes.*

Rackham You know what you're among, Read. Sailors who were treated like shit by the Navy. White labourers worse off than black slaves. Misfits, blokes out for a good time. A blotchy birthmark on the British Empire's spreadin' arse.

Mary So?

Rackham The arse's got a Navy, we just got each other. Equality, solidarity – our only strength.

Mary I know that.

Rackham I know you know. It shows. But you still make yourself out different.

Mary I don't try to.

Rackham What you got there?

Reaches towards MARY's *shirt.*

Mary (*backs off hastily*) Only paper!

Rackham What you scared of? (*Short pause.*) Why paper?

Mary Use my hands, should I?

Rackham No tinder.

Mary What for?

Rackham Signals.

Mary I'm not a spy.

Rackham Take it easy! (*Pause.*) Pirates' motto, that. If it's not easy, don't take it. Enjoy yourself! That's what we're in it for. Have a drink.

Offers her a flask.

Mary No thanks.

Rackham A pirate refusin'!

Mary I want to go.

Rackham 'Old on to it.

Mary I have been.

Rackham I got a ship to protect, Read, my men to think of. I'm only what I am 'cos they made me. I was quarter-master till our old captain Charlie Vane went yellow. Wouldn't tackle a French man o' war. More guns, more metal, but if we'd boarded, the best boys would've won. The boys thought we were best, and so did I. Made me Captain for that. But we still eat together, all take the same pay. A unit. We stick together. – Have it while I'm talkin', I don' mind.

Mary I like my privacy.

Rackham We noticed. Don' drink with us, don' screw. If you weren' so fuckin' good with that sword an' that pistol, they'd 'ave 'ad the bollocks off you weeks ago.

Mary Like to see 'em try.

Rackham So why are you in it?

Mary I'm not. I was forced into piracy. Yours was the first boat out of Providence, that's all. First place we stop, if it's not a jungle, I get off.

Rackham Scared of the rope, eh?

Mary The rope's all right. If it wasn't for the rope there'd be as many villains at sea as there are on land. Then we'd all be out of a job.

    ANN *comes on.*

Ann Jack!

Rackham Meanwhile, Read, you're a pirate like the rest of us. An' comin' t' the same rope's end.

Ann That you, Jack?

Rackham Over here! – Despise them, Read, you despise me.

Ann Jack, two of 'em down there set to kill each other. If you don't break it up, we won't have a crew left.

Rackham Fuckin' animals.

    He goes. Pause.

Ann Nice night.

Mary I came up for a crap.

Ann On your own again?

Mary I just had all that.

Ann Calls them animals, pissed himself half the time.

Mary Solidarity.

Ann Getting at you, was he?

Mary He thinks I'm a spy.

Ann I like independence. It's a sham, this . . . togetherness. You ought to stand up to him. You could put him down any time.

Mary I got nothin' against him.

Ann He picks on you.

Mary I'm the odd one out. He's Captain. It's natural.

Ann That's not what I'd call it.

Mary Anyway, he's got the power.

Ann Get organised then.

Mary I couldn't take him on.

Ann He's all show! Look at the clothes he wears! Striped trousers. 'Calico' Jack! Wears scent too.

Mary I noticed.

Ann All those rich women he's supposed to have had – all scrubbers. He was in service once, that's all. Stole the silver.

Mary I don't know why the crew put up with you two, the way you carry on. Why'd they allow you on the ship?

Ann I pull my weight. Always have done. They know that.

Mary And now they know *how* you pull it.

Ann They're slobs! When I think why I took to pirates, I reckon I've been had. Back in Charleston the men were like tied-back beanstalks. You saw a pirate there, he looked like Charlemagne. Good clothes, plenty of money, glowing with health. At sea though, they're like sheep. Noisy, smelly, huddled together. All they think about's their stomachs, their pricks and their stupid discipline. I don't call them men.

Mary I'm sure if you keep lookin'.

Ann I have been.

Mary You're Rackham's privilege. You make him different from the others, an' they allow that. But cheat him, you cheat them. First sign of trouble, he'd have you an' the bloke overboard.

Ann Equality – a smokescreen.

Mary Not because of that.

Pause.

Ann Where'd you learn to fight?

Mary In the army.

Ann Indian taught me. I like you.

Mary You'd better go back.

Ann I always tell a man if I fancy him.

Mary He'll be expectin' you

Ann I been with pirates since I was sixteen. Never met one too much for me.

Mary I don't need trouble.

Ann You can handle him.

Mary That's not the point.

Ann We got the deck to ourselves.

She moves closer.

Mary Don't touch me!

Ann What you scared of?

Mary Nothin'.

Ann It's easy.

Reaches for MARY's *crutch.*

Mary (*shying away*) Are you mad? He'll kill you! Women make trouble.

Ann What's the matter? I got the looks. I'm clean.

Mary I'm not interested.

Ann Why not?

Mary You don't excite me.

Ann I haven't tried yet.

Mary No-one touches me.

Ann What's so different about you?

Pause.

I'll say you're bent. Then they'll all be after you.
Mary No.
Ann Oh yes.

From behind, she reaches into MARY's *shirt.* MARY, *now resigned, doesn't move.*

Mary I'm a woman.

ANN *shoots away.*

Ann That's not funny.
Mary Catch me sayin' it is!
Ann I don't believe it.
Mary Suit yourself.
Ann I felt something.
Mary Me.

Pause.

Ann I believe you.
Mary Big of you.
Ann You might've said earlier.
Mary I didn't ask you to find out.
Ann You didn't stop me either.
Mary What difference would it make? You kept on.
Ann How was I to know?
Mary Too bloody eager, that's your trouble.
Ann The only bloke on the ship I fancied! I've got secrets too, you know!
Mary Like what?
Ann I've gone off Rackham.
Mary That's a secret?
Ann And I feel we're put upon.
Mary Who?
Ann We women.
Mary Rich or poor, pretty or plain?
Ann All of us.
Mary Some more than others.
Ann Why d'you say that?
Mary A minute ago I was just one of the crew. I had a place. Now, because of you, I've lost it. He'll string me up.
Ann Never.
Mary Or put me off. One woman's bad enough.
Ann He doesn't know yet.
Mary You'll tell him.

Ann I won't!
Mary One way or the other. You're bound to.
Ann Whose side are you on?
Mary My own. Breathe a word of this, I'll cut your ears off.
Ann You and whose army?
Mary I can do it. You know that.
Ann Like to see you try.

MARY *draws her sword.* ANN *backs off.*

Ann It was a joke! I didn't mean it. No swords.

MARY *advances on her.*

Kill me and Rackham'll quarter you.

MARY *stops.*

We don't have to fight.

ANN *advances.* MARY *stiffens.*

Ann Look, I'm unarmed. Fists if you have to. Nothing lethal.
Mary I'm finished, Ann. I'll never get to the mainland now.
Ann Why don't you trust me? Look, I've been alone on this ship since the
   first day. Now there's two of us. That binds us. We're allies.
Mary He'll kill me. He already thinks I break up the team.
Ann What kind of team is it excludes you and me? He won't know! It's our
   secret. Shake.
Mary Why?
Ann You never know what's coming next, right? If you sit at table with them,
   it could be champagne, it could be a hand up your skirt. If you lie down
   with them, you don't know what's going up you, or where it's going even.
   Always in the dark. Now we've got them in the dark.
Mary All I want is to get off.
Ann All right! Shake on that then.
Mary I don't know. It's different for you. Things come easy to you. Your
   scars don't go so deep.
Ann We're women, that's the main thing. Two of us, and they don't know.
   That's an advantage, we can use it.
Mary What for?
Ann Ourselves!
Mary I'm nothin' without them.
Ann You are! A woman. Like me.
Mary No, not like you. On my own I know what I'm fighting for.
Ann Look, what's your name?
Mary Mary.
Ann Shake, Mary.

MARY *lowers her sword and offers her hand.* ANN *takes it and twists her arm behind her back. She grabs* MARY's *sword and holds it to her throat.*

You're right. Things come easy to me. But you're not the only one can be tough. And we're too good to be enemies. So don't pull a sword on me again.

Mary I won't!

Ann You're too trusting, Mary. Fighting well's one thing. Fighting dirty's another.

She offers MARY *the sword. Instead of taking it,* MARY *butts her and the two collapse on the floor. They fight playfully and* MARY *finishes on top.*

Ann Ow!

Mary This what you mean?

Ann Catch on fast, don't you.

Mary I'll do, will I?

Ann Absolutely.

Mary Quite sure?

Ann Cross my heart.

They laugh. RACKHAM *comes back.*

Rackham What's goin' on?

Ann Jack.

Rackham What you two up to?

The girls get up quickly.

Ann Just mucking about, Jack. Little celebration.

Rackham What of?

Mary (*quick*) Nothin'.

Ann Nothing special.

Rackham What's your game, Read?

Ann I told you!

Rackham I knew you'd make trouble, Ann. If it's in trousers, it must be good. This is a pirate ship! You're my woman! The men allow me that because they trust me. What's goin' a happen if every Tom an' 'Arry can get it up you? Where's the trust then? They'll be fallin' over each other, fightin' for you. Chaos! The idea is to make life easy, not add complications.

Ann What's complicated about doing as you like?

Rackham There's never been a ship where a woman aboard didn't mean trouble, even one in chains, let alone a good-timer like you. I went out on a limb over this, an' now you undermine my authority! I've got to sort it out.

Draws his sword.

Ann Won't do it that way, Jack.
Rackham I owe it to the men.

He turns on MARY. *She backs off.*

Ann You owe them nothing! It's sheer jealousy, this!
Rackham Come on, Read, you're the arms expert.
Ann No, Jack! No sword!
Rackham What you mean?

Looks at his own sword.

Ann Read. He's unarmed.
Rackham So what? I want to kill 'im, not test my strength.

He lunges. MARY *dodges.*

Teach you unarmed combat in the army, Read?

He lunges again. MARY *dodges again.*

Ann She's a woman, Jack.
Rackham (*lunges again, then*) Eh?
Ann A woman.
Mary (*angry, to* ANN) What'd I tell you!
Rackham Who?
Mary Me.
Rackham What you talkin' about?
Ann It's Mary Read, not Mark. She just told me. That's what we were laughing about.
Rackham Christ almighty, Ann, you'll try anythin'.
Ann It's true!
Rackham He's killed more men than the rest of my crew together.
Mary When I first got captured by pirates, I was workin' as a seaman on a Dutch trader. The pirates said if we'd didn't join 'em we be stripped for valuables an' put ashore. I couldn't undress in front of men like that. I had no choice.
Ann Why d'you think she's always on her own?
Rackham Cos 'e's a pest.
Ann It's the truth, Jack.
Rackham Strip now, then. Prove it.
Ann Show him, Mary.

MARY *hesitates.*

Rackham Come on then, let's see!

MARY *still hesitates.*

What's the matter? Shy?
Ann Don't bother. He knows now.

Rackham A he or a she, I want to know!
Ann Lecher!
Rackham Strip or I'll run you through!

MARY *scoots to pick up her sword.*

Mary Try it now, I'll kill you.

RACKHAM *appreciates the difference.*

Mary I don't want this known.

Pause.

Rackham Havin' one's bad enough. I got more sense. Come on, you.

ANN *avoids him and moves closer to* MARY.

Ann Get stuffed.
Rackham Two of 'em now! Two bloody women! Decadence like creepin' rot!
Soon we'll all be in skirts!

He goes. ANN *laughs.* MARY *stares ahead, catching her breath. They sing:*

Ann	I've argued with men.
	I've told them they were wrong.
	But they never believed me
	When I was on my own.
	But now I've got an ally,
	A sister who's near me,
	When I open my mouth
	I know they'll have to hear me.
Mary	I've gone along with men.
	I thought they couldn't all be wrong.
	But they can't explain
	Why I was on my own.
	And now I've got an ally,
	A sister who is near me,
	When I open my mouth
	Will what they hear be me?
Both	Women! In a men's world.
	Poor! Amongst the rich.
	In: a dog eats dog world,
	Who thinks: about the bitch?
Ann	You can argue with me sister,
	But we do fight the same fight.
	And now that we're together,
	They'll have to see we're right.
Mary	I will argue with you sister,
	So we do fight the same fight.

> For now that we're together,
> We have to get it right.

Both   Women! In a men's world.
> Poor! Amongst the rich.
> In: a dog eats dog world,
> Who thinks: about the bitch?

They announce . . .

JULY 1720   ABOARD THE SHIP, OFF CUBA

. . . and go off.

Afternoon. Three of the pirate crew – NOAH HARWOOD, JOHN DAVIES *and* THOMAS EARL *stand around* TOM DEANE, *who is crouched trouserless on the deck. They prod him with their swords and try to lift his shirt-tails.*

Earl Where's 'er knickers then?

Davies Seen 'er frillies, 'ave you?

Harwood Bleedin' woman.

> EARL *waves* DEANE'S *trousers in the air.*

Deane I want them back.

Earl So you can run away again?

Davies You got a date with death, mate, an' you're keepin' it.

Earl 'Oo is she anyway?

Harwood Our pilot, ain' she.

Davies Navigatin' officer. Same as James Bonney.

Earl I never seen 'er do any navigatin'.

Harwood Won' co-operate, will she.

Deane I refuse to! I'm an officer of His Majesty's Navy!

Harwood No need to be a berk about it.

Deane I was forced on this ship! I am not a pirate!

Earl That's not your fault. You were keepin' the wrong kind of company, that's all.

Davies Yeh, losin' kind. Mush fer food, piss for booze, the lash fer wages an' scurvy fer a pension.

Harwood Think yourself lucky, Deane.

Davies Better standard of livin' now. More say in what you do. Yer own boss!

Deane I am not part of this!

Harwood You can say that again.

Davies 'Ead on 'is shoulders.

Earl Won' be there long once Blackie gets 'old of it.

Davies Crouched there like a fuckin' baby.

Harwood (*to* EARL) What would you do with no trousers?

Davies Wave it aroun', boy, I ain' ashamed of it.

Earl 'oo's 'er fella, anyway?

Harwood Mark Read.

Earl Readie? Get off!

Davies 'E's discipline personified. No-one touches 'im!

Earl An' this one's only been with us a week.

Harwood They been seen together. 'Oldin' 'ands by the foc's'le.

Earl Ah! True love!

Davies I don' believe it. Wouldn't 'ave none when I asked 'im. Turned nasty.

Harwood 'E obviously likes a bit of class.

Davies What d'you mean?

Harwood This is love, Davies. Not animal lust.

Davies Bloody cheek!

Earl What you mean love? Readie's the 'ardest case on the boat.

Davies An' a good crewman.

Earl Not a man t' cross.

Deane Please. My trousers.

Harwood When the others come. We're keepin' you 'ere till you fight.

Deane Please. I promise.

Earl 'E promises!

Davies Jump for 'em then. (*Takes the trousers from* EARL *and dangles them over* DEANE.) Up, boy, up!

Earl Careful, 'e bites!

Davies Up, boy! Jump!

MARY *comes on.*

Mary What's goin' on?

Earl Nothin', Readie.

Harwood Seein' what 'e's made of, that's all.

Davies If anythin'.

Mary Why you got his trousers?

Harwood 'E tried t' run away. So we took 'em off 'im. 'E's got a fight on.

Earl With Blackie.

Mary When?

Earl Now.

Mary (*to* DEANE) That true?

Deane Yes.

Mary How'd it happen?

Harwood 'E called Blackie an ape.

Mary So he is.

Harwood Blackie challenged 'im, an' 'e accepted.

Mary That's stupid.

Deane He insulted me!

Mary So what?

Deane I can't go on being insulted!

Mary Why not?

Deane He had no right!
Mary He's bigger'n you. With this sort survival comes first.
Deane I'm a navigating officer of His Majesty's Fleet!
Harwood Superior bastard.
Earl Steer a ship, but can't steer his cock.
Davies Keeps gettin' up the wrong kind of inlet!
Mary (*cold*) What did you say?

    Pause.

Davies Nothin', Readie.
Mary Give him his trousers.
Earl Don't you like him like that?
Mary Now!
Harwood Waste of time. Blackie'll cut 'em off again in no time.
Mary You heard me.
Earl Goin' a make us?
Mary (*draws sword*) Three of you?
Davies Yeh. All together.
Mary But you'll come one at a time. Same way you'll go.
Earl Not if I was behind you.
Mary Get there.

    EARL *realises he can't move alone.*

One at a time. Like I say.

    RACKHAM *comes on with* FETHERSTONE *and* BLACKIE. *Behind them* ANN *and*
JOHN HOWELL.

Rackham What's the trouble?
Mary No trouble, Captain.

    Sheathes her sword.

Rackham Come to watch, eh?
Mary That's right.
Fetherstone Your man ready?
Mary Who says he's my man?
Fetherstone No-one second him?
Rackham What about you, Howell?
Howell I don' want no part of it.
Rackham Why not?

    Takes HOWELL's *arm. Pause.*

Rackham That's up to you. I'm not 'avin cliques though.
Ann It's no clique. Just him and me.
Rackham All right, let's have you.

DEANE *and* BLACKIE *step forward. The others form a circle round them.*

Pistols first, swords after. No other rules. You give up or get killed.

Davies Guess 'oo 'e's talkin' to!

Earl 'E's shakin'!

Ann Call this a fight, Rackham?

Rackham Mind yer own.

Harwood Blackie'll slaughter 'im.

Fetherstone 'Is own fault if 'e won' co-operate.

Ann The bear and the mouse.

Blackie Get on me knees for 'im, shall I?

Mary It's not a contest, Rackham.

Rackham So what? This ain' sport, it's procedure. If a man insults someone, 'e's askin' t' get called. If the other man's bigger, that's 'is look-out. It's how we sort things out.

Howell It's not his way.

Fetherstone 'E's on our ship, 'e plays our rules.

Ann Didn't turn out the way you wanted, did he. Made a nuisance of himself.

Rackham What's that to you?

Ann Today him, tomorrow the rest of us.

Rackham The rest of us are different. No pirate fights 'less 'e knows 'e's goin' a win. If this man was stupid enough t' call Blackie, 'e deserves all 'e gets. I'm not runnin' a rest 'ome for retired government navigators.

Howell It was you retired 'im.

Deane This is pointless. I'll fight my own battles.

Ann You shut up. There's more than you involved.

Rackham All right. Ten paces.

FETHERSTONE *measures it out.*

Mary I got a bone t' pick with Blackie myself.

Fetherstone Ha!

Rackham Since when?

Fetherstone Since 'e found out about the fight.

Mary No, weeks ago.

Rackham Past 'istory, then.

Mary That Spanish brigantine. It was Blackie's turn t' go first. We agreed before an' paid him for it after. He didn't go. Just stood there.

Blackie That's a lie!

Mary Also, I wasn't told about this fight.

Rackham If you got a general complaint, make it official. If it's personal, this is how it's solved. Which d'you want?

Mary I just thought I'd mention it.

Howell What are we provin' 'ere? Blackbeard the Second's less yellow than the Navy?

Ann Just picks on its green bits.

Blackie I'll have you for afters!

Ann Just your style: women and children first.

Rackham Ready!

> DEANE *and* BLACKIE *are standing ten paces apart. They cock their pistols. The others stand well clear.* MARY *draws her sword, points it at Deane.*

Fetherstone What's that for, Read?

Mary I could run 'im through myself from here. Just as easy.

Rackham What's the matter with you? You know the drill.

Davies Can't face the thought of lonely nights, can you, Readie.

Rackham (*to* MARY) You want me to stop the fight?

Mary Blackie's makin' 'imself big on another man's hard luck.

Davies You mean you want to be the Big Man yourself.

Earl An' 'ave 'Ard Luck for the little woman.

Mary Shut up!

Rackham You want to fight Blackie yourself?

Mary I never said that.

Rackham If you do, fight him after. I'm not havin' a free-for-all.

Mary I don't want him second-hand.

Earl It's no sweat fer Blackie, Read. 'E's only got t' breathe on 'im.

Davies Time it takes, 'e'll be nicely warmed up for you.

Blackie I'll fight Read first.

> *Cheers from* EARL *and* DAVIES.

Rackham There's a personal difference to be settled. You can't change the rules just like that.

Ann Even when they're not working?

Rackham A free-for-all helps no-one. We're a small crew as it is, without decimatin' ourselves. An' over what? A man who's done nothing but sit on 'is backside since 'e joined us. 'E's a pain in the arse.

Earl Not in Readie's!

Davies You're breakin' a beautiful friendship, Captain.

Rackham All right, listen. If the rules are bein' questioned, you ought t' know the full score. Read's a woman.

> *Pause.*

Davies Do what?

Harwood You're jokin'.

Rackham Mary Read, not Mark. Ann knows. She found out.

Ann Rat!

Rackham True or false?

Ann True.

Harwood This on the level, Jack?

Rackham So she wouldn't be fightin' for herself. She'd be protectin' 'er lover.

Earl Stone me.

Harwood Can't see my old woman goin' that far.

Rackham I'll explain the position. We're a small crew, we need good men. I don't care about Read. We got one woman aboard an' that's trouble enough. But Blackie's one of our best men.

Earl So's she.

Harwood Right.

Davies That's not a woman.

Earl Show us yer tits, Readie!

Mary Shut up.

Fetherstone Whyn't you tell us before, Jack?

Rackham Read didn't want it known, an' I didn't want this 'appenin'.

Earl What?

Rackham Personal bickerin'.

Ann That what you call it?

Rackham It disrupts.

Ann What? Your authority?

Rackham Our unity.

Harwood So what we goin' a do?

Earl Let's see 'er fight.

Rackham I tell you, it's a waste. We're short-handed as it is. A government ship could pick us off just like that.

Davies Blackie can handle her.

Blackie I ain' fightin' a woman.

Harwood She can look after 'erself.

Howell That's what he's afraid of.

Rackham All right, no one fights nobody. Call it off.

Fetherstone If it's gone this far, Jack, it's got to be sorted.

Earl Yeh, we're expectin' it now!

Davies An' we want to see a fight, not a warm-up.

Ann (*ironic*) Captain says no, Captain's word's law.

Rackham Not if they don't agree.

Ann Chicken.

Earl We don't. (*Slight pause.*) Do we?

Davies Just cos there ain' a rule for it, don' mean it can't 'appen.

Harwood Vote on it.

Pause. RACKHAM *nods.*

Fetherstone For the fight?

Harwood Which one?

Fetherstone Deane an' Blackie.

He, RACKHAM, DEANE *and* BLACKIE *raise their hands.*

Against?

ANN, MARY, HOWELL, EARL *and* DAVIES *raise their hands.*

Fetherstone Noah?
Harwood The two fightin' are for it.

Points to DEANE *and* BLACKIE.

Fetherstone What about you?
Harwood Abstain.
Fetherstone Falls. Fer Read an' Blackie.

ANN, MARY, HOWELL, EARL *and* DAVIES *raise.*

Against.

He, RACKHAM *and* DEANE *raise.*

Earl (*seeing* DEANE) 'E's against!
Harwood Outvoted.

MARY *replaces* DEANE, *cocks her pistol,*

Rackham I tell you, it's unnecessary!
Fetherstone Fire!

MARY *and* BLACKIE *fire their pistols and miss. They draw swords and fight.* MARY *kills* BLACKIE.

Fetherstone (*to* MARY) Couldn't lose, could you.
Earl Big man.
Davies For a woman.
Harwood No one's goin' a rape her in a hurry.
Rackham Satisfied?
Mary I wanted it kept quiet. But you took my cover, and you nearly took my man. I just wanted to keep him.
Rackham You kept 'im. Like the wrong company you're keepin' now. You've split us right down the middle. Prey now for any government vulture roun' the next headland. The biggest mark we could've made was a scratch. Now we can't even make that. 'E's all yours.

They look at DEANE *who is standing apart from* MARY, *looking the other way.*

Harwood 'E don' look all 'ers.
Davies Which one's the woman?
Mary I kept him. Preserved. Like a pickle.
Rackham Throw this one overboard.

The pirates remove BLACKIE'*s body. Everyone except* MARY, ANN, DEANE *and* HOWELL *go off.*

Ann Now what?
Mary You get what you want, don't you.
Ann Don't you?

Mary It's all changed now. To keep him alive I killed what tied us.
Ann He's not even said thank-you.

DEANE *says nothing.*

Howell Tongue-tied.
Mary What can he say? No one knowin' kept us together. Now they know
I'm a woman, I can't be one.
Ann What'd you see in him?
Mary A man. Gentle. We'd settle down.
Ann He say that?
Mary Didn't need to. It's been in my head for years. Timber walls, smoke
out the chimney. By a river where I could do the washin'. Red hands.
Apron. Now the apron's leather an' the red is blood.
Ann They'll watch us like hawks from now on.
Mary Why? We've done our worst already.
Ann But not our best.
Mary I travelled three thousand miles for that apron. All I've got's a sword
an' a pistol. An' no use for either.

DEANE *walks off.* MARY *crouches, head in hands.* ANN *and* HOWELL *leave
her.* MARY *sings:*

We turn away, look for a new world,
And turn our back upon the old.
But all the time it's there behind us,
It pulls us back into the fold.

We run away and leave behind us
All that we hate and detest.
That's not to say it's been got rid of.
All that we've done is fly the nest.

Instead of having run away
We should've stayed and done away.
Kept the old enemy in view
Know where we're going's really new.

We band together in our new world,
Don't see we're still part of the old.
If we're not strong we'll just repeat it.
We'll keep ourselves within its hold.

She announces . . .

OCTOBER, 1720   THE SHIP OFF NEGRIL POINT, JAMAICA

. . . and goes off.

Evening. ANN, HOWELL, DEANE *and* MARY *sit in a group. They have been drinking.* ANN *is looking out to sea with a glass. The crew, who have been entertaining guests, are all thoroughly drunk.* DAVIES *and* EARL *sit together, as do* HARWOOD *and* FETHERSTONE. RACKHAM *sits with* JOHN EATON, *a turtler, one of the guests.*

Earl Whass the lady doin', John?

Davies Tryin' a scare us as usual.

Ann You scare yourselves, you don't need me. (*To* HOWELL.) It's them all right.

Howell Can't be.

Ann Government colours. Just ran 'em up.

Howell I can't see.

Ann Here.

Gives him the glass.

Mary This was supposed to be a quiet place. Safe.

Ann (*urgent, to* HOWELL) Tell Jack.

Mary An' get the others.

Ann What others? When the turtlers came aboard they broke open two barrels. They're all pissed out of their minds.

Mary What a mess.

Ann The last free ship in the Caribbean. Drown in booze or swing on the rope, it's all the same. There's only ourselves to live for.

Mary So we let ourselves get hanged.

Ann Not you and me. When'd you last have a period?

Mary I forget.

Ann If you're pregnant, they can't hang you. It's the law. They can't hang innocent life.

Mary Tell me now I feel guilty, won't you.

Howell Captain, government ship astern.

Rackham Piss off, Howell, I'm enjoyin' life.

Howell See for yourself.

Offers him the glass.

Rackham I'm entertainin' my friend the turtler, John Eaton. Say hello!

Howell I have done. Get up.

Rackham Howell, the only bad news you bring is yourself.

Howell Look, will you!

Shoves the glass on RACKHAM.

Rackham For trouble? Why should I? (*Looks.*) Oh Christ.

DEANE *comes over and takes the glass from him.*

Mary Shut your eyes an' it goes away. I thought that was our game.

Deane They've seen us. Thank God.

Mary You're the only one who does, Tom Deane.

Rackham Weigh anchor!

Ann What for?

Rackham We're gettin' out.

Harwood We only just cast it, Captain.

Ann We can handle them.

Rackham Weigh anchor, I said!

Earl Whass goin' on?

Rackham We're bein' chased.

Earl I was just gettin' settled.

Rackham Come on, Davies, look lively.

Davies Me, lively?

Earl 'E's put away enough t' drown the entire English Navy.

Davies Why not ask them? (ANN, MARY, *etc.*) They 'aven't even done their share of the drinkin'.

Rackham I'm not askin', I'm tellin'. That's a government ship an' they're after our necks.

EARL *starts to slink off.*

Where you goin', Earl?

Earl Home. My Dad 'ad a farm back in Devon. Borin' as sin. I ran away t' see life. 'Dead around 'ere,' I said. Can't get much deader'n we're goin' a be.

He goes below.

Rackham (*to* ANN) Completely demoralised! This is your doin'!

Ann Why us? We've got the will.

Mary Speak for yourself.

Rackham T' get it, you took theirs!

Deane They're coming about!

Davies Well, can't sit 'ere all night.

Rackham Where you goin'?

Davies Downstairs.

Rackham There's work to do.

Davies I'm not stoppin' anyone.

Rackham Noah, if anyone tries to leave, put a ball in 'is gut.

Davies What is this?

Rackham The real world. (*To* FETHERSTONE.) All hands.

FETHERSTONE *goes below*

Ann (*to* MARY) Come on, we'll show 'em.

Mary Show 'em what?

Ann Come on!

Mary I got things t' do.

Ann With him?

DEANE, *with the glass, is staring out to sea.*

Mary What else is there?

She stares at DEANE. RACKHAM *watches them.* ANN *slaps* MARY'*s face.*

Mary What's that for?
Ann Work to do. – Right, Captain?
Rackham Now the Arse is about to sit on 'er, she wakes up.
Mary You don't hit me, we're friends. I can put you down any time. (*She stands.*) Any of you!
Ann Grab hold.

She begins pushing the capstan.

Mary Why hit me?
Ann Push!

MARY *pushes with her.*

Rackham You two, get busy!

DAVIES *and* HARWOOD *join* ANN *and* MARY.

Rackham Howell, you got some climbin' t' do.
Howell Tryin' a get rid of me?
Rackham Also, I can't see anyone else.
Mary Push, push, an' still get nothin'.
Ann You've got all you'll get from Tom Deane.
Mary His kid, you mean.
Ann Make out that's his arm.
Mary Break!

She strains to push the capstan. FETHERSTONE *comes back.*

Fetherstone They won't move, Jack.
Rackham (*to* EATON) We need sail.
Eaton Not me!
Fetherstone Come on, off your backside!
Eaton I'm a guest. You invited us.
Howell Only at gunpoint.
Eaton We're not involved in this.
Rackham You're on my ship, you do as I say.
Eaton Supposin' they catch us? If we help, it's aidin' an' abettin'. They'll string us up.
Rackham Never.
Ann It's coming. (*The anchor.*)
Howell (*to* EATON) We'll speak for you.

Deane I never collaborated. Remember that.

> RACKHAM *turns suddenly and shoots at him. He misses, calms down, looks at* EATON.

Eaton Bad enough gettin' caught with you. Worse if we help you escape.
Rackham Get movin'.
Eaton We'll be garotted!
Rackham I'll do it for you now if you don' get up them ropes!
Eaton What's wrong with your crew?
Fetherstone Like raisin' the dead.
Rackham Go with 'em, George.

> EATON, HOWELL *and* FETHERSTONE *climb the ropes.*

Eaton I protested. Official.
Rackham Just get on with it. Noah, take the wheel. Keep as far from them as possible. They're takin' the near shore, you take the far.
Ann Anchor weighed, Captain.
Mary Up down, up down.

> *She and* ANN *finish raising it.* DAVIES *is sneaking off below.*

Rackham Davies, you and the women – ropes!
Davies In my state of health?
Rackham Get movin'!

> DAVIES, ANN, MARY *and* RACKHAM *stand by to fix ropes.*

Deane They're coming on fast.
Ann We can't not fight 'em.
Rackham Pirates fight for a reason. We've got none. Unless you want to make 'em madder.
Ann Just one shot.
Rackham One shot an' you'll feel the full weight of their metal. That boat's got guns like we got rats.
Ann You mean, ours haven't left.
Rackham Not for want of hintin'.
Deane She's beautiful!
Mary Huh!
Ann Just one shot, Jack. Show 'em we're not worried.
Rackham We are though. They're threatenin' our fun. And to keep it, we got to put ourselves out. It don't make sense.
Ann They'll skin us!
Rackham Not if they can't catch us.
Ann We're not even away yet.
Rackham (*shouts up*) What's wrong?
Ann Only three up there, that's what's wrong.
Rackham Noah: sail. I'll take the wheel.

HARWOOD climbs the ropes. RACKHAM *takes the wheel.* DEANE *goes below.*

Ann You start working when I do yours.
Rackham They've got the breeze off the coast.
Ann I can see their faces. One shot, Jack.
Rackham There's no point.
Ann They might turn tail.
Rackham I don't care either way.
Ann Right.

She prepares to fire a small cannon.

Mary Playin' with your balls again?
Ann Why should they spoil our fun?
Mary (*looking round for* DEANE) My man's gone.
Ann If he was a man, he wouldn't have gone.
Mary I don't believe they exist any more. Not around here anyway. If I have a boy, I'll bring him up as a girl. See how he likes that. (*Holds out her hand to an imaginary child.*) Keep your shirt down, Georgie, don't confuse people.
Ann You just going to stand there babbling?
Mary Tell me the answer then.
Ann Find your own.
Mary When you've got them all?

ANN *fires her cannon.*

We can't fight them!
Ann They've got no right!
Mary Have we?
Ann All right, it's just war.

Answering enemy fire, much heavier.

Rackham That's enough, Ann.
Ann They've got to see we mean it!

The four come shinning down the ropes.

Harwood Jesus Christ!
Howell You might've warned us, Ann!
Ann What you think I was doing? Stuffing a chicken?

More enemy fire.

Davies They're firin' back though!
Ann Of course they are! That's not just another unarmed merchantman. Their trade is murder!
Howell Oh Christ.

Goes to go below.

Ann Where you goin?
Howell Get my head down. This is too much.
Ann They've called us. You've got to have an answer!

More fire. Part of the rigging falls. HOWELL *goes below.*

Eaton This is dangerous.
Davies Permission t' go below, Captain?
Rackham Why not?

He joins them.

Ann Where you off to?
Rackham There's half a barrel untouched down there. Might as well be consistent.

More fire. More rigging falls.

Fetherstone Mind your heads!
Eaton Come on!

Everyone but ANN *and* MARY *goes.* ANN *takes the wheel.*

Mary Mind your head, Georgie.
Ann Look at it. Empty. Me, the night and a raving lunatic.
Mary Takes one to know one.
Ann Me? I couldn't be more logical!
Mary Nor could the others. Why are we different?
Barnet's voice (*off*) This is His Majesty's sloop 'Sarah'. Captain Barnet, commander. Who are you? Where are you bound?
Ann (*leaves the wheel and calls*) Jack Rackham! From the sea! Fuck off!
Barnet (*off*) I must call upon you to strike to His Majesty's colours!
Ann We strike no strikes!

Fires another cannon.

Mary You're mad!
Ann It's us and them.
Mary Always is. An' as usual they're stronger.

Answering enemy fire.

Ann We're mothers. They can't touch us.
Mary Try tellin' that to a bullet.
Ann Get the others back then.
Mary Men!

She goes to the hatch. More fire.

Bunch of grandmas! Where are you?
Earl (*below*) Piss off!
Davies (*below*) People down 'ere tryin' to sleep!

Mary They'll hang you!
Earl (*below*) Die 'appy!
Fetherstone (*below*) Bloody women!
Mary Whyn't you come up an' fight!
Howell (*below*) You come down! I got somethin' on 'ere worth fightin' for!

Laughter.

Mary Think I'm up here for my health!
Howell I'm up! I'm healthy!

Laughter.

Harwood (*below*) 'Is spike an' your marlin!

Laughter. A hissing sound. Balls fall on the deck. ANN *scuttles over to* MARY.

Ann Small shot!
Harwood (*below*) All big shots down 'ere!
Mary Call for quarter, Ann, for Christ's sake!
Ann They're coming from behind.
Howell (*below*) Any way you want it, my love!

Laughter. ANN *goes to the side, calls.*

Ann Jack Rackham from Cuba! We call for quarter!
Barnet (*off*) Lay down your arms!
Ann Load up.

She loads her pistol.

Mary What for?
Ann Pick a couple off as they come on.
Mary After we've surrendered? They'll murder us.
Ann What d'you think they're trying now?
Mary It's not honest.
Ann Only by *their* rules! When it gets dangerous, we stop!

They lurch as the ships touch.

Ann They've touched.
Mary Miserable worms!

Fires her pistol into the hatch.

Davies (*below*) Aagh!
Earl (*below*) What'd you do that for?
Ann Come on.
Mary How?
Ann Side each. Pick 'em off as they come. Then swords. Back to back at the
  end. Reload.

They take up their positions. MARY *reloads.* EARL *appears through the hatch.*

Earl You shot Johnny!
Mary P'raps now he'll wake up.
Earl We were in this together.
Mary That stopped months back.
Earl (*sees the approaching boarding party*) Oh Christ.

He goes back below. ANN *has a sailor in her sights.*

Ann Now!

She fires. A SAILOR *gets aboard. He wears a grey jacket, baggy red trousers, black and white striped waistcoat and check shirt – naval uniform. The* GIRLS *see him, then turn to look at each other. As the* SINGERS *come on, the scene breaks.*

Singers   So the women stayed to fight on deck
             While the men just hid below.
             For freedom lived in their bellies,
             And they'd stolen the men's long ago.
             So their enemy was laughing
             When he brought them in in chains.
             But inside the girls were laughing too,
             For they'd soon be free again.

             For it takes two to tell what's right and wrong.
             You can draw or cross the line.
             And if women make men children,
             It's their children make man-kind.

             Now when the girls were brought before the court
             The judge was a man called Lawes.
             The Governor of Jamaica
             Had decided to show his claws.
             He brought in all the pirates
             And condemned them to the rope.
             But one thing which old laws can't change
             Is that while there's life there's hope.

They announce . . .

NOVEMBER, 1720 ADMIRALTY COURT, SAINT JAGO DE LA VEGA, JAMAICA.

. . . and go off.

Bench, dock, witness stand, seats for the public. ANN, MARY, RACKHAM *and* EATON *in the dock.* GOVERNOR LAWES, ALEXANDER FORBES *and* WILLIAM

NORRIS as judges. DEANE *sits amongst the* PUBLIC *but near the witness stand.* CAPTAIN BARNET *and* TWO SOLDIERS *stand by the* PUBLIC, *heavily armed.*

Barnet (*reads aloud*) By virtue of a commission from His Majesty King George . . .

Man in Public 'Ooray!

Barnet . . . pursuant to an Act of Parliament entitled 'For The More Effectual Suppression of Piracy' . . .

Low hisses from PUBLIC.

. . . for the adjudging of all piracies committed within the jurisdiction of this Admiralty Court before His Excellency Sir Nicholas Lawes . . .

Murmurs and low hisses from the PUBLIC *as the names are announced.*

. . . Governor of Jamaica and Chief Justice, Alexander Forbes, Receiver of His Majesty's Revenue and Provost Marshal, and William Norris, Collector of Plantation Duties and Register, you John Rackham, Ann Bonney and Mary Read . . .

Wild outburst of cheers and applause from PUBLIC.

. . . are charged . . .

Lawes Captain Barnet, can you bring the court to order, please.

BARNET *signals to his* SOLDIERS *who thud their musket-butts on the floor, then aim them over the* PUBLIC'*s heads. They go quiet.*

Barnet . . . are charged that you did piratically board a sloop of unknown name belonging to persons unknown to this court, did put its master Thomas Spenlow in fear of his life and did steal the said sloop and tackle to the value of three hundred pounds.

Murmurs and whispers from PUBLIC.

And you, John Eaton, are charged that you did feloniously go over to the said prisoners, at that time notorious pirates and known by you to be so. The session is resumed.

Lawes Prisoners at the bar, you have heard once again the charges against you, and you have heard the evidence of Master Spenlow and Captain Barnet in support of them. Do you have any further questions to ask these witnesses?

Silence.

Or any witnesses to produce on your own behalf?

Silence.

Or anything to say in your own defence?

Eaton Governor sir, me an' the turtlers, sir, we're innocent. We just bought a pettiauger t' go turtlin' off Negril Point. Rackham an' his crew pull alongside an' ask us t' drink with 'em. We said we'd sooner not . . .

Man in Public When'd you ever turn a drink down, John?

Eaton Shut up, this is serious! – Only then they pulled guns on us, see. Then when Captain Barnet's sloop attacks, they couldn't get their own men to hoist sail, so they threaten us if we don't help 'em. We weren't in league with 'em, sir, an' we didn't help of our own free will.

Rackham I'll second that.

Mary They had to help us. The crew were too bloody pissed!

Laughter from PUBLIC.

It's true! They were forced! Like I was!

Lawes Mistress Read, do you have any witnesses or evidence to support your assertion?

Mary (*to* DEANE) Tom, you tell him.

Lawes Do I understand you wish to call Master Deane as a witness?

Mary Yes.

Lawes Step forward please.

DEANE *steps forward to murmurs from the* PUBLIC.

Mary You know the turtlers were forced, Tom.

Deane I don't.

Mary You were there!

Deane I saw them come aboard with Rackham. I saw them drink with the crew. That's all.

Mary But they're not pirates! You know that!

Forbes When Captain Barnet attacked, Master Deane, what did the turtlers do?

Deane They helped hoist sail.

Forbes Would you say their behaviour was at any time that of men acting under duress?

Deane No, sir. They seemed very friendly towards the crew.

Ann Bastard!

Mary They were forced at gunpoint! Like I was!

Forbes Mistress Read claims she too was forced into piracy.

Mary You know how it happened, Tom. I told you.

Forbes Can you say that Mistress Read seemed at any time unwilling to be aboard the pirate ship?

Deane No, sir.

Mary Tom!

Ann She saved his rotten life!

Woman in Public Bloody turncoat!

Man in Public Save 'is own neck, though!

Barnet Silence!

Lawes Thank you, Master Deane.

DEANE *steps down.*

Ann I'll tell you how it happened, Governor. She was passing as a man in the crew of a Dutch merchantman when they were attacked by pirates. What would you do if a hairy brute of a pirate stuck a pistol under your nose and said, 'Strip or join us?'

Murmurs of agreement from PUBLIC.

Old Woman I'd say I'll strip *and* join you!

Laughter.

Barnet Silence!

Lawes Mistress Bonney, we are not concerned here with *how* Mistress Read or Master Eaton became pirates, but only with the charges against you. Captain Barnet has described how yourself and Mistress Read were the only two to offer resistance to capture. And we have Master Spenlow's description that you were both 'very profligate, cursing and swearing much, and ready and willing to do anything on board'.

Rackham They were. I once asked Mary if she was afraid of hangin'. She said if it wasn't for the rope, our profession would be overcrowded.

Laughter from PUBLIC.

Mary I said there'd be as many villains at sea as there are on land. An' I wan't 'alf right!

Ann Yes, how can you accept Tom Spenlow's word and not Eaton's, Governor? Spenlow's drunk as much with us in his time as Eaton.

Mary Spenlow's no angel. When we borrowed his boat, he couldn't have been more obligin' if he'd wrapped it in ribbon an' given it as a Christmas present.

Ann Why call one a pirate and not the other?

Lawes Mistress Bonney, we are not here to provide a definition of piracy. Only to answer the charges before us.

Ann Sea-artists is what we are. No different from the rest of the Caribbean – Governors and Navy included!

Cheers from PUBLIC.

Rackham We just sailed around, keepin' ourselves in what we needed to live. We never stole except face to face with people where we were answerable to 'em. We never attacked anyone 'cept in self-defence. I mean, you got to protect yourself. Can't trust anyone these days, can you, Governor.

Laughter from PUBLIC.

Barnet Order! Order!

Rackham I mean, you sent Barnet's sloop out attached sky-high with cannon an' small arms. What for? A tradin' voyage?

Barnet We had to be able to defend ourselves. I've even heard there are pirates in these waters.

Laughter from PUBLIC.

Rackham Like I say, you can't trust anyone. But I've heard somethin' too. That your ship, Captain Barnet, was armed up on the anniversary of King George's coronation. Right?

Lawes Is this getting us anywhere, Master Rackham?

Rackham I don' know about us, but you've done all right out of it!

Laughter.

Rackham You paid for those arms, Governor, from his (*referring to* FORBES) taxes and his (*referring to* NORRIS) plantation duties. That's money from the people of this island, to protect what? I'll tell you. The court says the owner of Tom Spenlow's sloop is unknown. But Tom was here testifyin'. Why didn't you ask him?

Forbes We need only ask questions relevant to the charges, Master Rackham.

Rackham Who told Spenlow to testify against us?

Forbes No one needed to tell him. You stole a ship and tackle from him.

Rackham Not from Spenlow. It wasn't his ship. No skin off 'is nose what went missin'. But for the owner i'ts a different matter. Why isn't the owner in court?

Lawes Master Rackham, if you'd wished, you had the opportunity to find the owner and bring him to court.

Ann What opportunity?

Lawes Also to question Thomas Spenlow.

Rackham Why should I land Tom Spenlow in it just to bring his (*referring to* FORBES) brother-in-law to court?

Eaton He's the owner?

Rackham His brother-in-law.

Uproar from PUBLIC.

Barnet Order! Order!

No effect. BARNET *instucts his* SOLDIERS, *who fire their muskets over the heads of the* PUBLIC. *They fall silent.*

Lawes If there is a repetition of these outbursts, the court will be cleared. Now, Master Rackham, I've said before and I'll repeat: your line of argument is not relevant to the charges.

Rackham Never mind that. You represent King George on this island,

Governor. But you also depend on the planters and the traders. And they can either vote for the Crown or against it. You spent the people of this island's money to protect his brother-in-law's trade, which the people of this island never see a penny from! Everyone's bein' rooked here, an' we're the scapegoats! Revenge, that's all this trial is!

Ann Call us pirates, they probably got three brace of pistols under those gowns!

Laughter from PUBLIC.

Lawes Master Rackham, you were told before we resumed that you may not challenge the authority of the court. If you have nothing more to say, the court will be cleared while the judges consider their verdict.

Ann (*to* RACKHAM) If we'd thought, we could've organised this.

Rackham Don't you talk to me about organisation.

Barnet The court will rise!

The PUBLIC *are cleared out by* BARNET *and the* SOLDIERS, *except a* YOUNG CREOLE WOMAN *who hovers behind, unnoticed at first. Dark and seductive, she fans herself.*

Lawes Damn nerve.

Norris What've you been up to, Nicholas?

Lawes They'll think up anything. And it's always the same argument. Leech off the community, tar your witnesses with their own brush, then play to the gallery. It's time we held these trials in camera.

Norris Not if you're using the island's money to settle private scores.

Lawes It was Barnet's idea!

Forbes Bright chap, young Jonathan.

Norris Set a rat to catch one.

Lawes Rackham's been a damn nuisance, William. They've positively terrorised the settlers on the north coast, not to mention the interference with trade.

Norris George's in particular.

Forbes The fact that he's my brother-in-law is neither here nor there. It could've been anyone.

Lawes (*notices* CREOLE WOMAN) Is she staying?

Norris I brought a couple of bottles. I thought, if this was going to be a long session . . .

Lawes Is it?

Norris Rackham's no fool, and nor am I. Assembly's paying eight thousand a year for the protection of England's armed forces.

Lawes Does your wife know about her?

Norris Sorry, sweet. Later.

CREOLE WOMAN *smiles and goes.*

Not an English Presence, gentlemen, but delightful all the same.

Forbes I don't see it makes a great difference who owned Spenlow's boat.

Norris You two play it really close, don't you. Alex with his brother-in-law. And you, Nicholas, is this the fourth blue-blooded widow you've married? Even she's beginning to look a bit sickly. You must have more in-laws in England's aristocracy than I've got slaves.

Lawes I don't think you're terribly well placed if we're to discuss our private affairs, Bill.

Norris A whole dynasty from a few coffee beans!

Lawes I'm concerned for the continuing prosperity of the whole island, that's all.

Norris Which island?

Lawes The fortunes of England and Jamaica are inextricably linked.

Norris You mean because Alex spends more time hanging round their parliament that he does ours.

Forbes I find the climate here oppressive after a few months.

Norris So you go back to Bristol and tell your magistrate friends to send more scum out as cheap labour.

Forbes A black riot every fortnight this summer on the plantations. We must have some sort of . . .

Norris Buffer. I heard it was because you felt insecure you weren't bothering to cultivate any more. Just leaving land idle so the price rose. Then some poor bugger buys it off you, tries cultivation, and you bankrupt him.

Lawes What's your point, Will?

Norris Who's paying and what for, that's my point.

Lawes It was George last autumn, it could be you next spring. Piracy affects us all. (*Pointed.*) We do have to be unanimous on this, you know.

Norris I'm not arguing with the verdict. But like Rackham I prefer to know how it's being reached.

Lawes Guilty then. And Eaton? I thought there might be some doubt in his case?

Norris Don't be hypocritical, Nick. In these cases it's our word against theirs. And with a crowd like that watching, we need to set an example. They're all the same once they get together anyway. Hang one, hang the lot.

Lawes Our argument is nothing if it's not just. It's worth taking time over this.

Forbes No, Will's right. We're getting nothing from pirate traffic just now, except trouble. It's time we took a firm stand.

Lawes You both say guilty then.

Forbes Yes.

Norris. Guilty.

Lawes So be it.

Norris Drink?

Offers LAWES *his bottle.*

Lawes No thanks. I want to get this over quickly – Captain Barnet!

BARNET *comes in.*

Everyone back in, please.

As the JUDGES *return to their seats, the* PIRATES *come back on and the* PUBLIC *resumes its former position.* BARNET'*s* SOLDIERS *strike the floor with their musket butts.*

John Rackham, Ann Bonney and Mary Read, you are found guilty of the felonies charged against you.

Mixed reaction from PUBLIC.

John Eaton, you are also found guilty as charged.

Unrest amongst the PUBLIC.

Mary But he's innocent!

Lawes Does any of you have anything to say why sentence of death should not be passed upon you?

Ann The human tanner – hang 'em up and cure 'em.

Lawes John Rackham, Ann Bonney, Mary Read and John Eaton, you will go from here to the place whence you came, and thence to the place of execution, where you will be severally hanged by the neck till you are dead. And God have mercy on your souls.

Rackham Oh Christ.

Ann If you'd fought like a man, you wouldn't have to die like a dog.

Lawes Remove the prisoners.

Ann Your Excellency, just a minute. You can't hang us two.

Lawes Mistress Bonney, once the law has run its full and proper course, it can hang whom it pleases.

Ann Sod your law. We're pleading our bellies . . .

Lawes Mistress Bonney, hunger is no justification for a felony. Even the most extreme circumstances could only mitigate the sentence.

Mary We're not hungry, love, we're up the spout.

Laughter from PUBLIC.

Man in Public You did get something done then, Jack!

Forbes D'you mean you're pregnant?

Ann Our only defence: womanhood. We've been chased from pillar to post, didn't fit in here, didn't fit in there. But we did find one place for ourselves. As mothers. You can't hang innocent life.

Rackham The same law of England that hangs men like dogs lets bitches keep their litters.

Mary You watch your language.

Lawes (*to* FORBES) Is this true?

Forbes I'm afraid so. Of course, they'll have to be examined.

Ann The law knows better than us of course. We've got the proof inside us, but you have to tell us. And after you've discovered we're right, we'll still be carrying it. But there still won't be a place for us, and there'll still be some man telling us he knows better.

Mary Me, they told I was a boy. Ann, they told she was a lady. If everyone tells you lies, you've only got yourself to go by. You get to be your own judge. Only all the judges are men. (*Looks at* RACKHAM.) His crew should've helped us, but it didn't. So in the end it catches up with you: what can you do on your own?

Rackham Get nowhere fast.

Mary There was only one man I trusted. And he's long dead. The rest was a waste of time.

Ann Hang us pregnant, you hang innocence. Hang us after, you deprive innocence. Either way we got the truth on us, and your law can't touch it!

Lawes Clear the court!

BARNET and the SOLDIERS do so. Again the CREOLE WOMAN stays behind

Brazen bitches!

Norris Where's your argument now?

Forbes We'll need a doctor.

Norris To prove them right? Try the one you bankrupted. He could do with the work.

Forbes None of us is in charity.

Norris That's right. A dead hand. At least with them (*referring to the* PIRATES) there's something growing.

Lawes (*stands*) And with us. I suggest, gentlemen, we sink our differences in a bottle from Alex's new crop.

Forbes Fine. (*To* NORRIS *as the* CREOLE WOMAN *takes his arm.*) We like a fresh opinion on our new blends.

As they go, the SINGERS come on and sing:

Singers   So the case was stitched up tight
And England's growth was still called free.
But Lawes had been made impotent
By the pirates' potency.
And though Rackham died on the gallows,
And his crew went the same way,
Their story stayed behind them,
Remembered to this day.

Sugar and spice and all things nice
That's what England was made of.
The rich drew the line and didn't think twice.
All around the world
Sugar and spice and all things nice,
But not for little girls.

Now Ann went back to Charleston
Or so the stories say.
She'd had her fling with piracy
And skipped, unscathed, away.
But Mary died of fever
In her damp cold prison cell.
Which if her child had its mother's luck
Was maybe just as well.

Sugar and spice and all things nice
That's what their world was made of.
But it came at too steep a price
For these little girls.
No sugar, no spice, you have to think twice:
About another world.